A Lady Never Tells

A Lady Never Tells

LADY BE WICKED
BOOK ONE

DAWN BROWER

"...when pain is over, the remembrance of it often becomes a pleasure."

— JANE AUSTEN, PERSUASION

Contents

This is a work of fiction. Names, characters, places, and incidents are products of the author's imagination or are used fictitiously and are not to be construed as real. Any resemblance to actual locales, organizations, or persons, living or dead, is entirely coincidental.

A Lady Never Tells © 2023 Dawn Brower

Cover art by Mandy Koehler Designs

For all those that find strength when they need it most. Do not give up. You never know what you might discover in the middle of your journey.

Prologue

Her anxiety had hit an all-new level. Eden Barrett, the Countess of Moreland, did not take risks. It went against her very nature to do so, yet that was exactly what she was about to do. She'd willingly accepted an invitation to the Duke of Sinbrough's masquerade ball. It would be like literally entering into a den of iniquity: Sin itself on full display at this ball. The duke was infamous for having the most debauched parties for anyone who wished to attend. It was rumored even the most strait-laced ladies would don a mask and join the festivities.

She should be all right. Shouldn't she?

If she kept telling herself that, then perhaps she would. She'd convinced her good friend, Mrs. Claudine Grant, to attend the masquerade with her. She'd even commissioned scandalous costumes for them both. Eden's gown was the pure white of innocence, but it was anything but that. It was made for sin, and she hoped she would live up to the invitation it presented.

Her mask was also white to match the gown, but it had ruby red feathers fastened to it on one side and a little splash of color to show she wasn't as innocent as the dress may suggest. Just in case the low-cut bodice didn't do the job. She had left her golden-blonde hair loose and flowing down her shoulders. Her mask kept them from going wild, but if it was removed, then they might just become unruly.

"Are you ready?" Claudine asked.

"As I'll ever be." She smiled at her. Eden tried to embrace her inner wickedness, but so far it seemed hidden. "Someone is about to approach us." She nodded slightly in the direction of two gentlemen making their way through the crowd. "I do believe the gowns are working." She'd had Claudine's gown designed in a decadent pink that nearly matched her friend's skin tone.

Claudine grinned. "One of them is the man I hoped to see tonight. I'd recognize him anywhere."

"How fortunate that he's noticed you as well."

When the two men reached their side, Claudine's love interest stared at her briefly before he held out his hand and said, "Dance with me." Claudine went off with him, willingly leaving Eden alone with the other gentleman.

"Would you like to take a spin around the floor?" the other man said.

There was definitely something sinful about him. His hair was as black as his clothing, and his eyes a gorgeous green. She tilted her head to the side and studied him. "You're the Duke of Sin, aren't you?"

"Was I being too obvious?" He grinned. "Would you like me to live up to that moniker?"

Eden wasn't interested at all in him. He might be sexy as, well…sin, but she didn't find him all that interesting. She wanted to *feel* something. She didn't know exactly what, just that he did nothing for her. She shook her head. "No, thank you."

Someone laughed from behind her. "Have you lost your touch, old man?"

The Duke of Sinbrough frowned. "Don't be ridiculous. That would never happen." He wiggled his eyebrows at Eden as if that said everything. "We're just becoming acquainted."

Eden turned around to glance at the man who had just entered behind her. He didn't wear all black like most of the men in the room. However, he had not bothered to wear a waistcoat and jacket. He had on dark blue pantaloons and a stark white shirt, but no cravat. He had left his shirt open, giving her a marvelous view his neck and part of his chest. The gentleman was completely disheveled. His hair wasn't nearly as dark as the Duke of Sinbrough's. It was more brown than black, but his eyes were a similar shade of green. Where she had found the duke's pretty, this man's were filled with heat.

That heat spread over her like a whirlwind. She'd been looking for someone to spark something in her. Eden had started to believe she couldn't feel true passion. What was it about this man that made her want more? Was this desire? How had she never felt anything like it before? She took a step toward him and tilted her lips upward into what she hoped was a wanton smile. "Do you think you can do better?"

He returned her smile, and it sent shivers right through her. "I know I can," he told her. "Would you like me to try?"

"You mean you haven't already?" She tilted her

head to the side. "Wasn't that what you were doing when you slid your way behind us?"

He chuckled softly. "You may be right." He leaned forward and said in a demanding tone. "I want you?"

"Do you?" She licked her lips. "I might let you have me." She stepped closer and trailed her finger over his collarbone. "But the night is still young. I have many options. What makes you my best choice?" The Duke of Sinbrough had been forgotten. She didn't even bother to see if he was still standing nearby. This man...he made her body come alive, and she wanted him.

The Duke of Sinbrough sighed... "I know when I'm not wanted. I'll leave you two to your dalliance." Good. She didn't need two men fawning over her. Eden might not survive the night. One man was more stimulation than she could bear. It was best that Sinbrough made his leave. She turned her attention back to the stranger before her.

She'd never flirted like this in her entire life. Eden felt alive for the first time. The thrill of this was beyond even her wildest imagination. He stepped closer until her breasts rubbed against his warm chest. Her nipples tightened at the mere hint of his heat, and the pleasure was intoxicating. He leaned down until his mouth was near her ear. His breath caressed her skin, making her even hotter with need. "Darling," he said in a husky tone. "You've already decided. Don't make me beg."

Her throaty chuckle sounded foreign to her ears. Who was this wicked, wanton, widow allowing this unknown gentleman to seduce her? She didn't recognize herself, but wasn't that why she'd come to this masquerade? She slid her hand down and pulled out his shirt from his pantaloons, then slid it underneath until her fingers met his naked flesh. She trailed her fingers up his chest and then around his waist. He yanked her closer. "You're playing with fire, love."

"But what a burn it'll be," she replied in a husky tone. "You did say you wish to play with me tonight. Dazzle me with your skills."

"It'll be my pleasure," he said as he lowered his mouth. When his lips touched hers, she forgot everything, even her own name. *Yes.* This was what she had come to the masquerade for. She hadn't known what she'd been looking for until he'd come near. Damn, this was good, and she suspected as the night rolled on she'd experience more passion than she'd ever known in her marriage.

She wanted this man, and she'd have him.

Then, after this night she would go back to the proper Countess of Moreland. She had to keep up appearances, after all. There were people that depended on her. But for this one night she could have him and all the pleasure his kiss promised. No one else had to know. A lady never tells her secrets, and this one she would always hold dear.

One

A bead of sweat trailed down Eden's forehead. She wanted to wipe the moisture away, but her hands were otherwise occupied. They were, in fact, full of bolts of fabric she desperately wished to place somewhere else. Roslyn, her sister-in-law, was currently being fitted for several more gowns for her debut season. The shopping seemed to be never ending, and all Eden wanted to do was hide away in her sitting room and read. The idea of the upcoming season distressed her. She didn't like the *ton* or society, and had never had a debut season of her own.

"Are you certain you wish to have gowns made from all of this?" Eden lifted the bolts so Roslyn could see them. "You already have…"

"I don't have enough gowns. Do you have any sense of the amount of balls, soirees, and picnics we are about to be invited to?" Roslyn lifted a brow. "More than even I can imagine, and I can picture many." The girl sighed. She was standing in the center of the seamstress's dressing room while the woman frantically pinned her hem in place. "I have been waiting so long for this, and I do not want to be a failure because I lack the necessary attire."

Roslyn had a similar coloring as Eden. They could be mistaken for sisters in truth, and not just by marriage. Though Eden was a head shorter than Roslyn, they both had golden blonde hair. Their eyes were both a light shade, but Roslyn's was blue and Eden's green. "I understand that you feel you're at a disadvantage." Eden didn't get to finish her thought before Roslyn turned her head to glare at her.

"My brother is, was, a fool," she said with enough vehemence to slice a person to ribbons. "His death, while unfortunate, was easily preventable if he'd had the good sense to use the intelligence his birth had given him."

"Some might say that his lack of intelligence is what led to his demise," Eden said drolly. Her marriage had not been a love match. Her father, and the late Lord Moreland's father, had wanted the union. Neither of them had been given a choice. Perhaps, if love had been a part of their marriage, William never would have strayed, and with Eden's dearest friend at that. She'd lost her friend and her husband in one act of selfishness.

Roslyn laughed. "I shouldn't find that funny," she said between chuckles. "But there is too much truth in that statement to ignore its veracity." Roslyn took several deep breaths in an attempt to get her laughter under control. "In all seriousness, most gentlemen don't stop to think about how an amorous affair might lead to disastrous consequences. My brother was more foolish than most. Not only did he tup his best friend's wife, that very wife was your friend too. How did he not realize that was a horrible decision?"

Eden shrugged. "I stopped trying to deduce the inner workings of your brother's mind many months ago." While she'd been grieving the loss of her reputation more than his death. The *ton* spoke about her in hushed tones that were not as hushed as they thought them to be. Eden didn't know if Roslyn realized how much the *ton* gossiped about their family, and that it might make her chances of finding a husband harder than it should be. Even though they were about to enter society and it might be a battle, Eden was determined that Roslyn would not have a husband like William. One of them should find a gentleman who believed in marriage and love. Eden had given up on that for herself. It was enough that she didn't have to worry about how she'd survive and that her young son would always be safe.

"Set that fabric over there," Roslyn gestured with her hand. "I've already discussed with Madam Broussard what type of gowns I would like. She'll know what to do with them." She smiled. "I hope you have had some new gowns made as well."

She had, but not nearly as many as Roslyn had ordered. "I won't embarrass you."

"You never would." Roslyn's smile faded. "You're too young to be alone. You should reconsider your decision to never remarry."

Roslyn was only four years younger than her. Eden had turned three and twenty a couple months earlier, and she couldn't imagine ever trusting another man with her life again. She was finally free from the dictates of a man, and she had some trusted friends, widows like herself, she could rely on. Eden didn't need to remarry. "I am content with my life."

"But we're finally out of mourning…"

"And that's a good thing. It allows you to have your debut now. It is enough that you wish to marry, and we will ensure you have a good husband." One that wouldn't be unfaithful and hold her in the highest regard. "I'm happy with my circumstances." She smiled as brightly as she could, even though she didn't feel particularly happy at that moment. Eden was hot and irritable. All she wanted to do was go home and rest. It had been a trying day. "Don't distress yourself unnecessarily. I promise I'll be all right once you marry and move away."

Roslyn stared at her for several moments in silence, then nodded. "Have it your way. The lord knows you always do. I swear you've become more stubborn since William's death." She tilted her head to the side. "I suppose that was bound to happen, wasn't it? His actions, while shocking, affected us both in ways neither of us could have foreseen."

"That they did," Eden agreed. William had always been selfish, but that had been the worst thing he'd ever done, and it had led to his death. "At least he had the good sense to ensure we are both taken care of, and that Caden has a suitable guardian for his estates until he reaches his majority." Eden had funds of her own, so she didn't need to seek anything from her son's guardian, Roslyn had a dowry set up by her father, but William had added to it. It was almost as if he had known his scandalous behavior might prove a detriment to his younger sister.

"I'm done with the hem, Lady Roslyn," the seamstress said. "We can remove this gown and then start on the next one."

Roslyn nodded, and the seamstress helped her out of the gown. Eden sighed. This afternoon would never end… She would survive it, though. Roslyn depended on her, and she wouldn't be another selfish person in the young girl's life. Neither of them had a parent they could rely on. Roslyn was already in the next gown with the seamstress pinning where the alterations needed to be made when Eden snapped back to attention.

"Is Claudine going to visit again soon?" Roslyn asked.

Claudine Grant was another widow who had befriended Roslyn. She had come to visit while they prepared for Roslyn's debut season. She had left when her husband's father noticed her in Hyde Park. Since Claudine avoided her father-in-law, she had bolted. "I think she is to return soon." There would be a meeting with other widows that Claudine would need to attend at the Dowager Countess of Wyndam's in the next week. "But I don't believe she'll be coming to Moreland House."

"Oh," Roslyn said, a little crestfallen. "I like her. We should at least invite her to dinner."

That was a splendid idea, but she didn't know if Claudine would want to stay in London long. She would likely wish to return to the widows' estate, Matron Manor, that the Widow's League owned. Eden had been invited to join the league after William's death, and it had been her saving grace. Amongst other widows, she'd discovered what she truly wanted for her life. Recently, she had even been bold enough to attend a masquerade filled with scandalous behavior. Her cheeks heated as she remembered that night. It was one she would never forget, and also never tell another soul about. It was her secret. One she relished more than she wanted to admit. "I can invite her, but I cannot guarantee she'll accept."

"All we can do is ask," Roslyn replied, then shrugged. "I do hope she accepts, but I understand if she cannot."

Eden smiled. Roslyn was very much unlike William. He was selfish and only thought about himself. His sister was kind and loving. How could two siblings be so dissimilar? She hoped that Caden wouldn't be anything like his father. It was her job as his mother to ensure that he would make better choices. Her son was her sole focus. "I'll send her a missive when we return home." Eden was almost certain she was already at Lady Wyndam's, but even if she wasn't, she would be soon.

Roslyn nodded and returned her attention to the seamstress. Eden found a nearby chair and plopped down on it, overheated and exhausted. After this fitting, they should be ready for the season. If only Eden was prepared for the vacuous gossip of some of the *ton's* leading matrons…

MAX HOLDEN, THE DUKE OF CARRINGTON, STARED down at the missive on his desk. His mother was being her normal tedious self… She didn't come to town often, but apparently, she was going to deign to present her person in London, and soon. It was enough to drive a man to drink. Especially when his mother decided to meddle, and she most definitely intended to.

Apparently, she had decided it was time that Max found a wife. While he understood the reasoning, and happened to agree with her, he'd never admit as much to the woman. She would become even more unbearable then. He didn't want a wife, but he knew he wanted one. He had become guardian to his niece, Sarah, over a year ago. She'd been young enough that having a nanny to take care of her had been adequate, but now he realized she needed more than that. The little girl required a mother.

Which meant he would have to marry. He cursed his brother for dying. Sarah's mother, Caroline, had died giving birth to her. Caroline had never known her mother, and Max's brother, Owen, had barely paid any attention to his daughter. He'd drank himself into oblivion every day after his wife's death. If Max hadn't hired a nanny for Sarah, he doubted Owen ever would have. His brother had lived that way for several years before his behavior had caught up with him. He'd had one too many glasses or decanters of brandy and went riding in a storm. The horse had become spooked and thrown him. Owen's neck had broken on impact.

Sarah had become his responsibility the moment she'd been born, but he'd been able to pretend for a time it hadn't. He had hired the nanny and went about living his life. Now he had to find a bloody wife so his niece could have a mother. He ran his hand through his hair and blew out an exasperated breath. He didn't want a wife. But when had what he wanted ever truly mattered?

He had too much responsibility in his life, and it had started before he even reached his majority. His father died when Max was barely five and ten. He'd never attended school beyond Eton, and had taken his place as the new duke immediately. His family depended on him. That was his duty, and now finding an appropriate wife was another task expected of him.

Perhaps he should have a few drinks himself. He shook that thought away. Max rarely overindulged in spirits. He had learned that lesson when his father, then brother, had died from too much excess. *Hell.* What was he going to do? Max gave in and poured two fingers of brandy into a glass. One drink wouldn't hurt…

"What are you brooding over?" Emmett North, the Marquess of Crawford, said as he sauntered into the room. "Pour me a glass, would you?"

Max shook his head, but did as his friend asked. He handed Crawford a glass of brandy, then sat back behind his desk. He set his own brandy down and asked, "Why are you here?"

"I heard you attended the Duke of Sinbrough's masquerade a little while back," the marquess said in a casual tone. Max just stared at him. There was never anything casual about his friend. He was asking for a reason, but he didn't know what it could be.

"That was six weeks ago," he said. He kept his tone as neutral as Crawford's had been. He didn't want to let anything slip. "I've attended before."

"Not very often," Crawford replied, then sipped his brandy. "What made this one different?"

Damn… His friend was right. He hadn't gone to one of the Duke of Sinbrough's debauched events in quite a while. For the most part, it wasn't his type of ball. Honestly, no ball was one he liked to attend, but it had been important to him to go that night. It was when he first realized he would have to marry soon. It was like his last night of decadence before becoming the man who would soon have a woman he called his. He would never tell Crawford all of that. His friend would make it out to be something bigger than it actually was. He shrugged. "It seemed like a good idea at the time."

"And you don't think you should have gone now?" He lifted a brow. Crawford was mocking him, and he didn't know why.

"What are you really asking me?" Max didn't have the patience for games. There was too much for him to decide, and the marquess wouldn't let this go easily.

"I heard you found yourself a woman." Crawford sat up straighter. "A blonde goddess that Sinbrough wanted for himself."

Max grinned at that. He had spent the evening with a blonde and it had been memorable. So much so that he'd thought of her every day since. It was too bad he didn't know her identity. He wouldn't mind a few more nights with her before he found himself a suitable wife. "The Duke of Sin unquestionably wanted her for himself." Max shrugged. "She hadn't been interested. The lady definitely had more refined taste."

Crawford barked in laughter. "Sinbrough does spread his love around more freely." He lifted a brow. "Who was she?"

He frowned. She hadn't told him her name, but he knew almost every inch of her body. Her mask had covered nearly her entire face. "I don't know."

"How is that possible?" Crawford downed his brandy, then grabbed the decanter to refill it. "You did spend the entire evening with her, did you not?"

He had… "I fell asleep, and she left before I

awakened." Max really should have insisted she tell him her name. He'd been more inclined to ravish her at the time, though. "She never removed her mask. It's not like I attend those masquerades very often. I doubt I would know most of the people there." Or at least recognize them… "Some ladies prefer that their identities remain unknown."

"That is true," he agreed. "However, most of them at least tell their lovers their given name. This one didn't share at all?"

"No." He didn't need the reminder that he'd blundered. Max had given her pleasure, but he'd lost his mind when he'd seduced her. All he had been focused on was her and her delectable body. She'd been so bloody perfect. "If I could change that, I would. Why do you ask?" He hoped Crawford didn't want to bed the woman himself. He might have to beat his friend senseless if he did. Max thought of her as his, and yes, he knew he shouldn't. She didn't belong to him, but his desire for her was not yet quenched.

"It's probably nothing," he said. "I heard a rumor you were looking for a wife, and then, in the same discussion, the gentlemen were discussing your night at the masquerade. Some are wondering if you intend to marry her."

Max laughed. The gossip that went around the *ton* could be ridiculous. "I do intend to marry," he told his friend. "It is time. Sarah needs a mother."

"But since you don't know Lady Seductress's name, you can't very well marry her." Crawford grinned. "I don't envy you searching for a suitable wife. Do you have anyone in mind?"

He shook his head. "None." He sipped his brandy. It burned as it traveled down his throat. "I have requirements, though."

"As you should." Crawford grinned. "Care to share them?"

"She has to be beautiful," he said. "If I have to marry, I want to like actually looking at the woman."

"That goes unsaid," the marquess agreed. "And the rest?"

"She should be biddable. I don't need a woman harping on me daily." That sounded like a damned nightmare. "I don't need an heiress, but I suppose it wouldn't hurt that she didn't need to marry me for my fortune." What else? "She also has to be kind and capable of loving a child that isn't hers. I won't have her neglecting Sarah when that is the very reason I am even considering marriage."

"So, to summarize," Crawford began. "You do

not want a simpering young miss or an acerbic bluestocking, but something in-between. One with beauty and a flush dowry."

He glared at his friend. "You make it sound as if my list isn't attainable."

Crawford rolled his eyes. "Because none of those young debutantes are going to show you who they really are. All they will see is your title, and they'll pretend to be the type of woman you want. The only things on that list of yours you will be able to check off immediately are the beauty and the dowry. You're going to need help with the rest."

Bloody hell… "Are you volunteering?"

Crawford wrinkled his nose. "I'll speak with Lyonsdale. Between the two of us, we can uncover the rest. Just let us know which young ladies catch your attention, and we will investigate them for you."

"Thank you," he told his friend. The Earl of Lyonsdale, Crawford, and him had been inseparable since they met at Eton. "I appreciate your assistance in this." Max's wife would have to be the most suitable woman he could find. His young niece had enough upheaval in her young life. He lifted his glass. "To finding me a wife."

Crawford held up his glass. "To surviving the season."

They both drank the rest of their brandy, then set down their glasses. It would be an interesting season. Crawford had that last bit correct. There wasn't much that slid past the marquess. He had an uncanny ability to see through everyone and everything.

Two

It was the day of Roslyn's debut ball. They had attended an afternoon picnic that Lady Seabrook hosted earlier that week, but other than that, Roslyn had not been officially launched into society, and still Eden fought exhaustion. Preparing for Roslyn's launch had taken its toll, and Eden feared she'd be too weary to do much at the ball. Not that she expected to actually enjoy the festivities. She'd be too busy ensuring everything went smoothly for Roslyn. Eden couldn't wait for this event to be over so she could, well, not relax, but perhaps breathe a little easier. For now, though, she had mere hours before guests would start arriving. She just needed a few more moments to herself before then.

She'd unlikely relax fully until the entire season came to an end, and if Roslyn failed to secure a match, it would only all begin once more the following year. She didn't know if she hoped that Roslyn found a suitable gentleman to marry or if she prayed she never did. After Eden's own disastrous marriage, she was too bitter to not have a prejudiced view on the entirety of it all.

"Lady Moreland," a maid said as she entered the parlor.

What could possibly have gone wrong now? It seemed like something did as soon as Eden took a moment to herself. "Yes, Mary?"

"You have a visitor," she said. "Do you wish for me to show them in here?"

A visitor? That didn't seem at all like something good. Who the blazes was visiting now? Why couldn't they wait to speak with her at the ball? On second thought, perhaps it was good they had arrived before the townhouse was packed with people. If this was another issue, she'd rather handle it sooner rather than later. "Who is it?" She had to know who to expect in order to prepare herself.

"It's Mrs. Grant, my lady."

Eden let out the breath she'd been holding.

That was the best news. "Yes, show her in and have tea brought in." They would have a friendly visit, and she could inquire if Claudine could join them for dinner, as Roslyn had suggested. She'd forgotten to send a missive to her.

Claudine entered the parlor and stopped in front of her. "Pardon my intrusion." She grinned. "I do understand the importance of this evening. I expect you're quite busy."

"I am," Eden replied, then returned her friend's smile. "Not that my current circumstances portray that fact." She gestured toward the chair across from her. "Please, join me. I've sent for tea. You will stay awhile, right?"

"I will," Claudine said, "at least long enough to visit and have tea. I have news I wish to share with you."

It was so nice to have a friendly face to gaze upon. She'd been handling everything all on her own. Originally, Claudine had been supposed to help. That was before her father-in-law had spotted her at Hyde Park. "I hope you're not still hiding from Lord Artcrest."

"Actually," Claudine began. "I am not. That is part of my news. I no longer have to remain in hiding for fear he might force me back to his estate."

"Is that so?" Eden sat up straighter. "What has happened to change that?"

"I'm to be married," Claudine announced. Her smile widened at her news. Eden's heart fell. She didn't understand why this made her friend so happy. Hadn't she sworn she'd never marry again?

"I don't understand," Eden said. "I didn't think you had any suitors, and you were not in search of any. Is he forcing you to wed?"

If the Viscount of Artcrest was making Claudine marry, she'd help her friend. They were both widows and part of the league. Claudine's husband had died in the war. At least he'd had a noble death, unlike Eden's promiscuous husband. Was it any wonder she was so bitter?

Claudine shook her head. "Artcrest is not making me marry anyone, but he does approve of my marriage prospect."

Eden narrowed her gaze. "Then I fail to see why you are marrying. I'm afraid you must explain it all to me. This is rather confusing."

"I understand how it might be. I've been quite vocal about my wish to never marry again." She sighed. "But everything has changed. I'm in love, truly in love, Eden. He makes me incredibly happy."

This was terrible. "You thought you loved your lieutenant too," Eden reminded her. "Why is this different?"

Claudine drew in a breath. "You're right. I did." She nibbled on her bottom lip. "How can I explain in a way you'll understand?" She shook her head, then met Eden's gaze. "You're not even asking who I'm to marry?"

"Does that actually matter?" Eden wasn't sure it did. She had little faith in men in general. "I suppose to you it does. Who is it then?" She realized she was being rude, but she'd never been more surprised in her entire life. Claudine was going to marry again. Claudine. The one widow she would have bet never would. The world was upside down and she did not know how to right it again.

"I'm going to marry the Earl of Wyndam," she said.

Eden flinched. "The Dowager Countess of Wyndam's grandson?" She pushed her eyebrows together. "The one she has claimed to be a confirmed bachelor. How…"

The more Claudine told her, the more confused she became. If Lord Wyndam was going to marry her… Could he be trusted? Would he do to Claudine what Eden's husband had done to her? She prayed he'd be faithful to her friend, but she'd learned from experience that men couldn't be trusted.

"Do you recall that masquerade we attended?" Claudine asked.

"I do." Eden's cheeks heated as she recalled that night. She'd done some rather scandalous things that evening. All of which haunted her every day since. Some of her dreams were filled with what she had done, and she couldn't forget, no matter how hard she tried. The man she'd been with… He still haunted her dreams, and sometimes her waking moments. "What of it?"

"I spent the evening with him there." Claudine's lips twitched. "But to be honest, what started between us began much sooner than that. We gave into our desire that evening, and I do not regret it. I love him, and he loves me. I promise I am not entering into this marriage lightly. It is what I want. Can you be happy for me?"

She'd be awful if she couldn't support her friend. Just because her husband had been unfaithful didn't mean Lord Wyndam would do the same to Claudine. "If you're happy, then yes, I'm thrilled for you. When is the wedding?"

"Hudson, Lord Wyndam," Claudine began. "Is going to get a special license. It would be—" She coughed into her hand lightly. "—prudent for us to marry as fast as possible."

Was she implying what Eden thought? "Are you?"

"*Enceinte?*" Claudine supplied. "Yes."

"I see." She did, more than before. Even if she didn't love Lord Wyndam, she had a child to think of. Though Eden did believe Claudine thought she loved the earl. "So how soon is this wedding?"

"In a few days," Claudine told her. "I would like you to attend."

"Of course," Eden said automatically. "I wouldn't miss it for anything." She pasted a smile on her face. She would be happy for her friend. At least as long as she was in Claudine's presence... "Just tell me when and where, and I'll be there."

"I'm so glad," Claudine said. "You're a dear friend, and I do wish to share my special day with you. This is more exciting than my first wedding. I've never felt this happy in my entire life." She frowned. "When I married James, I was young and foolish. I did not know what it was like to truly love someone. I wanted to love him, so I convinced myself I did. This, what I feel for Hudson, is so much deeper. It's…consuming."

Part of Eden was jealous of her friend's newfound love. She'd wanted that for herself once upon a time—back when she believed in such fairy-tale notions. Eden wanted to believe in love again, but she had grown too cynical from her disastrous marriage. At one time she would have given anything to feel that deeply for someone. Would she ever know true happiness? The love she felt for her son would have to be enough.

"That's a blessing," Eden said softly. "I admit it is unexpected, but I couldn't imagine anyone more deserving of this happiness than you." Eden leaned forward and pressed her hand to Claudine's. "You're one of the best people I know. Do not let anyone take away what brings you joy. I'm glad you have something good in your life. No one merits it more."

"I could say the same about you," Claudine told her. "You've lost much too."

"But I've always had control of my life. That was taken from you." Eden fought tears, and she didn't quite know why. "Your heartbreak was real. Mine wasn't the same."

"But you had heartbreak, regardless of what caused it. We both lost someone, just in different ways. Your husband wasn't your person. Yes, he died, but his affair with your friend was the true betrayal. That loss cuts deep."

Yes, it did. She would never be able to forgive Claire, Lady Harewood. She'd been her closest friend since they were mere girls. Now she never spoke to her again. "That's true," she said that more to herself than to Claudine. Eden shook her head lightly. "There's no turning that clock back, though. We must move forward. I hope you'll attend tonight. Bring the earl with you. I'd like to judge for myself that he loves you."

Claudine laughed. "I would love to attend, and I will have Hudson escort me."

"Good," Eden said. "It'll be a grand event with you there."

"It'll be grand regardless if I attend or not."

Eden didn't have time to reply. The maid brought in tea, and they talked until Claudine had to leave. She still had a lot to prepare for anyway, and with Claudine's news, she had a lot to consider. Could she be as happy as her friend now was? She doubted it. It was best she kept to the path she'd carved for herself, and her heart was better kept protected. There was only so much it could take before it collapsed completely.

MAX STARED AT THE CLOTHING HIS VALET HAD LAID out before him. He still couldn't believe he was going to attend a debut ball for one of the young misses about to be launched into society. This was not how he'd foreseen his days going. He still had no wish to actually marry. Perhaps, before he dressed for the bloody ball, he'd pay a visit to the nursery. To remind himself of the reason he was going through with this farce.

Yes. That was a damned good idea. He left his bedchamber and headed to the nursery. His niece, Sarah, had just finished her bath and sat on a stool as her nanny combed her wet, brown curls. "Ouch," she said. "You're pulling too hard."

"My apologies, Lady Sarah," the nanny said. "But you've gotten your hair into a fine, tangled mess. I'm combing through as carefully as I can."

Max leaned against the doorframe and smiled. She was an adorable little cherub. He adored her and he would do anything for that little sprite. Sally, the nanny, finished untangling Sarah's hair and then plaited it. "There you go," she said.

Sarah popped her thumb into her mouth and sucked on it. "No," Sally told her. "Young ladies do not suck on their thumbs."

"I do," Sarah exclaimed around the thumb in her mouth.

Sally frowned. "It's time for you to go to bed."

Sarah turned and finally noticed Max. She leapt from the stool and ran toward him. In her excitement, she forgot the need to suck her thumb. Sarah launched herself into his arms. He chuckled as he swung her upward. Max hugged her against him. "Are you here to read me a story before bed?" she asked.

"I hadn't planned to," Max told her. "I'm going out for the evening."

Sarah frowned. "You never go out. Why are you leaving now?"

He did stay home each night since she had come to be in his care. Except for one, but his niece didn't know about that night. She had still been at his country house then. He had only recently had her moved to London so he could watch over her better. She needed stability, and he intended to ensure she had it. He would do anything for her, which was why he was going wife hunting.

"I may go out from time to time," he told her. "You'll be all right here with Sally."

Sarah wrinkled her nose. "I don't want you to leave."

Max could understand why she would be wary about him leaving. She'd been pretty much abandoned by her parents, and all she had left was Max. As if he didn't need a reminder of his responsibilities… This was why he'd come to the nursery. He would endure these society functions for her. She would never be left alone again. "I have to go out," he said, and then grinned. "How about that story, then?"

"You're going to tell me a story?" Her green eyes brightened at the news. Max could deny her nothing. If it made his niece smile, he'd ensure she had whatever her heart desired.

"I will," he said. "As long as you promise to be good for your nanny. It is your bedtime, and you will follow the rules that are set for you."

Her bottom lip popped out. Lately Sally had been having difficulty keeping Sarah in bed. The nanny would believe the little urchin was asleep and leave the room for a brief moment, only to return and find Sarah's bed empty. Then the entire household would have to search the townhouse for her until they found her hiding place. It was becoming frustrating. Max did not know why Sarah kept hiding from them. He didn't know what he could do to make her understand how terrifying it was to not be able to find her. She was so young, and it was hard to get through to the girl.

"Do I have to?" she pouted.

"Yes," he told her. "That's the price you have to pay for your story. Now, do you agree?"

"All right," she conceded. "But the story has to have a princess."

"Doesn't it always?" He lifted a brow. Max set her down. "Now climb into bed."

Sarah ran over to her bed and climbed in. Sally pulled up her bedspread until it covered the little girl. The bedspread had been made especially for Sarah. It was a patchwork of pieces of clothes taken from all her mother's gowns. She had never known her mother, but this gave her a piece of the woman who'd given birth to her. There were other things that he'd give Sarah later, when she was old enough to appreciate them. Pieces of jewelry, a journal, and a miniature of her mother... She was too young to understand their importance, but the quilt was something she could have now.

"I'm ready," Sarah announced.

"Are you?" He laughed. She was too precious for words. "Then I suppose it is time for that story you demanded." Max sat down on the edge of the bed and pressed the quilt around her. "You wanted a princess, right?"

"I do," Sarah said.

He nodded. "Once upon a time, in a land far away lived a princess…"

"How far was the land?"

"Is this your story or mine?" he asked.

"Mine," she said after careful thought. "But you can tell it."

He chuckled. "Thank you for giving me permission." He leaned down and pressed his lips to her cheek in a light, affectionate kiss. "Now, where was I?"

"A land far away," she reminded him.

Max grinned. "That's right." He tilted his head to the side. "The princess loved adventure, but her parents wouldn't allow her to leave the castle, so she made a wish."

"Did it come true?" Sarah asked.

He tapped his finger on her nose. "If you keep asking questions, I won't be able to finish the story."

She sighed. "All right, please tell me about her wish."

"The princess wanted to have the grandest adventure, but she didn't know how to ensure her dream would come true. She glanced up at the sky and saw a twinkle against the night sky." Sarah stared at him expectantly when he stopped speaking. His heart collapsed at all the loss this young girl had suffered already. "She stared at that twinkle and made her wish, but she didn't realize that twinkle wasn't the star she'd believed it to be."

"What was it?" Sarah said excitedly.

He stared at her until she pressed her lips together. Then he began again, "It was a dragon."

Sarah gasped. "Did it breathe fire?"

Max shook his head, and she became silent once again. "It was a magic dragon," he told her. "It granted wishes and offered to take the princess on an adventure, but she would have to leave her home forever."

"Did she go with the dragon?" Sarah asked quietly.

He shook his head. "She wanted an adventure

more than anything, but it was a price she wasn't sure she could pay. What would happen if she never saw her parents ever again? Would they forget about her?"

"They wouldn't," Sarah said emphatically. "They love her."

"They do," he said. "The dragon offered to take them with her too, but her parents refused. They told her that if it was an adventure she needed, she should go. They wanted her to be happy, and if she should return one day, they would happily welcome her home."

Sarah nodded. "So, she went with the dragon."

"Perhaps," he said. "We will learn more tomorrow when I tell you what happens next."

His niece pouted. "I want more now."

"No," he said firmly. "You must sleep, and I have to leave." He still had to dress for the ball. He tapped her chin. "I promise we will finish this story."

"All right," she said. "I cannot wait to hear about their adventure."

Max smiled softly. "Good night, sprite," he told her. Then he left her alone with the nanny for the evening. He prayed that the ball would go well. This need for a wife was trying, and he wanted it done as fast as possible.

Three

The carriage rolled to a stop before the Moreland townhouse. Max grimaced as he saw the line of carriages outside the window of his carriage. Everyone in the *ton* seemed to have been invited to this debut ball. What was so special about the young lady it was for? He should have asked Crawford when the marquess had suggested he attend. His friend had better show to the ball. He'd promised that he would bring the Earl of Lyonsdale with him, and they would assist Max in weeding out this year's crop of marriage-able misses.

He sighed. It was time to exit the carriage, but all he wanted to do was return home. It was imperative he attended this ball; he reminded himself.

Max needed a wife, and Sarah needed a mother. As much as he hated this, he had to do it. He *could* do it, and if he kept telling himself that, he might even convince himself of it, too.

Slowly, he pushed open the door of the carriage. He didn't want to wait for a footman to do it for him. Now that he'd decided to stick to his original plan, he didn't see any reason to delay. The sooner he was inside, the quicker he could peruse the young ladies in attendance. One of them had to be suitable, and one surely would meet his requirements…

Max stepped out of his carriage and strolled up the stairs to the entrance of the townhouse. A butler greeted him and motioned for him to follow some other guests to the location of the ballroom. He was early enough that he would still be announced, but too late to have to endure the receiving line. He hadn't really wanted to meet the hostess for the evening. She wasn't a lady he would consider marrying, anyway. The debutante was the one he had come to peruse, and he wanted to do that at a distance. If she interested him, he'd ask to be introduced, but not a moment sooner than that.

He reached a footman and handed him his

card. Not long after, the footman called out his introduction, "The Duke of Carrington."

After his name was called, he descended the stairs into the ballroom. Everyone turned to watch him make his entrance. He should have foreseen that. They would all clamor to be near him now. He never attended balls. That didn't stop anyone from inviting him to their entertainments. The society matrons would probably wonder why he had accepted this invite. What was it about this debut ball that had interested him? Some would conclude correctly that he was in the market for a wife, and then he would be swarmed. Hell, he would be anyway, but their avaricious intentions would be unavoidable.

Max turned left of the stairs and in the opposite direction of the dance floor. He had no wish to dance. At least not yet… Maybe he would later if he found a young lady he wished to be acquainted with more. He'd hoped that there would be a card room. It would give him some place to hide from the marriage-minded mothers in the room. They would stick to their younger charges and push them toward a potential duke with as much force as possible. They would all be eager to catch his attention. It was irritating, but his title could be quite the albatross at times. That made it impossible for him to know if a woman wanted him or if she hoped he would make her his duchess.

"You made it," Lyonsdale said from behind him. He turned toward the earl and grinned. His brown hair was a bit unruly, and his blue eyes nearly sparkled with mischief. "Crawford didn't think you would actually come tonight."

"Why?" Max grimaced. "He knows why I'm here."

"You're brave for attending this ball." Lyonsdale shrugged. "This is the start of your downfall. You do realize that, right?"

"What is it about this ball that requires bravery?" It didn't seem any worse than balls he had attended in the past. "And yes, I do know what this all means. It is a necessary evil." He'd brave the pits of hell itself for Sarah, and a *ton* ball was damned close to it.

"You don't recall what happened to the Earl of Moreland, do you?" Lyonsdale lifted a brow. "This shouldn't surprise me. You pay little mind to gossip."

"Because it is all a bit of nonsense." He shrugged. Max hated gossip. He thought only the worst sort of individuals partook in it. "Why should

I care about what happened to the Earl of Moreland?"

Lyonsdale chuckled. "You will. Especially if you become interested in his sister. This is her debut ball."

Max frowned. "All right, tell me. I suppose I should be aware of what everyone is discussing. Especially if I cross paths with the man."

"You really are out of touch." Lyonsdale shook his head. "The earl died well over a year ago."

Hell. He really should pay more attention to things. That was an important detail he should have been aware of. "Right. I suppose his death was shocking then."

"That's one way of putting it…" Lyonsdale glanced around him and then leaned in closer. "He had an affair with his wife's friend, and then the woman's husband killed him. It was all accidental, I've heard, but still shocking, as you guessed."

Max shook his head and repressed a groan. What a mess. "I suppose they're all waiting for the sister to do something equally shocking. Is that why this is such a crush tonight?"

Lyonsdale nodded. "The scandal has touched them both. They're not outright snubbed, but the *ton* doesn't look favorably on them either."

This was why he did not socialize much. Just because the Earl of Moreland had been foolish in his habits did not mean that, by extension, his family acted the same way. He would not pass judgment on his sister for what he had done. He couldn't help wondering about the wife, though. Had she known about her husband's proclivities? He would have to wait and access the dowager countess himself.

"I suppose I should say some pleasantries to the hostess and be introduced to the debutante." Max frowned. "I don't know how long I am going to stay tonight. Is Crawford here?"

"He's in the card room." Lyonsdale frowned. "You don't think he'd actually come out here, do you? He hates balls as much as you do."

"I'm glad there is a card room." He could retreat there later. "But go drag him out. I need to talk to him. Have him meet me by the hostess. Surely one of you can make introductions." He glanced around the room. He wasn't certain he knew who the hostess was. "Which one is she?"

Lyonsdale laughed. "You're hopeless, you know that?"

"Just show me." He didn't have the time or inclination to humor his friend.

"She's over there," Lyonsdale gestured to the other side of the dance floor. "And you're in luck. The debutante is with her. I don't suppose you wish to know her name?"

"That would be helpful." He should have known already, but he hadn't cared to pay any attention to the invitation.

"Lady Roslyn Barrett," Lyonsdale supplied. "I'll go retrieve Crawford now. Tread carefully, my friend. Lady Moreland is kind, but she also won't let you be rude."

"I'll be on my best behavior." He didn't bother looking at Lyonsdale as he spoke. "Do hurry with Crawford." He didn't want to be in the company of the young widow and her marriageable sister that long.

Max crossed the room and stopped before the two women. Neither glanced at him. They were both engrossed in conversation. It gave him a moment to study the two of them. They were both blonde and quite lovely. They were close in age. Lady Moreland was indeed a bit young for a widow. He also didn't understand why her husband had been unfaithful. She was a beauty, and there was something about her. He couldn't pinpoint exactly what it was, though. He cleared his throat, and they both looked at him. Lady Roslyn was beautiful, too. They could almost have been sisters, in truth. "My apologies," he said. "I arrived late and hoped you wouldn't mind my rudeness in introducing myself."

"We're aware of who you are, Your Grace," Lady Moreland said. Her lips formed a thin line. She didn't like him? What had he done to her?

"Then you have me at a disadvantage." He turned toward Lady Roslyn. "Has your dance card been filled?"

"It has, Your Grace," she said apologetically. She looked serene as she answered him. But he wasn't fooled. A hint of a mischievousness filled her gaze as she glanced toward her chaperone. "But you can dance with Eden."

Lady Moreland's mouth fell open in shock. "Roslyn," she chastised her. "That's completely unnecessary. I do not need to dance."

Eden... He liked her name. She didn't want to dance with him, and that made Max want to dance with her even more, and that surprised him. It was perverse of him, but he could be contrary. "I'd be happy to sign your card, Lady Moreland." He didn't give her a chance to argue with him. He lifted her card and scribbled his name on the first waltz. If he was going to dance, it would be one that he could hold her close. He wanted to unnerve her, and it would give him time to discern what it was about her that seemed so bloody familiar. "Until our dance." He bowed and left the two ladies alone. Crawford and Lyonsdale were nearby, and he walked toward his two friends. Perhaps they knew more about the countess. He'd have to ask for more details on the young widow.

EDEN COULDN'T BELIEVE ROSLYN HAD JUST DONE that. "How could you?" she hissed out. "You know I had no intention of actually dancing tonight." Especially with him… She'd recognized him immediately and her entire body had flushed with need. One he could, and had fulfilled in the past…

Roslyn shrugged. "He's a duke. One of us had to dance with him, and my card truly is full. It wouldn't do to snub him."

She closed her eyes and prayed for patience. Eden hadn't expected him to attend the ball. Everything she knew about the Duke of Carrington suggested he did not attend social functions. From what she understood, he hadn't actually attended one of Sinbrough's masquerades in a while, either.

It had been a chance meeting, and now he was here again. Why was fate continuing to throw him in her path? She had wanted to avoid him for as long as possible, hell, forever if she could have managed it. Now she had to dance with him…

Of course, a dance wasn't nearly as intimate as what she had already done with the man. He knew her body, and she was very much acquainted with his. Did he know who she was? Had he realized she was the woman he'd thoroughly seduced all those weeks ago? She hoped not… That would be disastrous. "I'll dance with him," she said in as even a tone as she could manage. Eden wasn't over him. The shadows of her night with him still danced in her memory. "But never volunteer me to dance again. I don't want a husband, and dancing is not something I've ever enjoyed."

"You should not close yourself off to the possibility of happiness," Roslyn said in a quiet tone. "I don't want you to live your life and regret what you could have had later. All I'm asking is that you consider opening yourself up to something more."

"I cannot make a promise I may not be able to keep," Eden told her. "I can't be hurt like that again. If I loved someone…" She swallowed a lump in her throat. "It would break me if they did not meet my expectations." Eden never asked for anything, and she realized now that had been the problem all along. She should ask for a great deal. If she were to open her heart again, she wanted more than the mediocrity that she'd had in her marriage. She wanted passion, love, and forever. In short, she wanted a man's full heart and attention. She wanted a great love that rarely happened, but everyone dreamed about. Even if they never wanted to admit it to anyone, especially to themselves.

"Just try," Roslyn said. "Start with a dance and see where it leads."

Roslyn did not know what she was asking of Eden. She'd already had a night of passion with that duke. If that hadn't opened her up to the possibility of something, more than a mere dance wouldn't change anything. "All right," she conceded. "I'll consider it."

"That's all I ask," Roslyn said. "Now I think my next dance partner is approaching. Be kind to the duke. He seems nice enough."

Eden hoped Claudine would arrive soon. She didn't know how much more of this she could take. She glanced around the room and breathed a sigh of relief. Her friend was here, and her earl was with her. Eden sucked in a breath. The way the Earl of Wyndam glanced at Claudine… He clearly adored her. Now that was apparently a great love match, and neither cared to hide it. Eden was envious…

Claudine and the earl walked toward her. When they reached her, Claudine grasped her hand. "This is a success."

"It is," Eden agreed. She hadn't expected so many to actually accept the invitation. "I wonder if they hope a new scandal will erupt on the dance floor. They're trying to hide it, but I think that is why they're all here. My husband's scandalous death was the talk of the *ton* for quite some time. Surely, by extension, Roslyn and I are equally sinful."

"They're fools," Wyndam said. "I wouldn't pay them any mind."

Easy enough for him to say… "I'll try." She didn't see any reason to be rude to the earl. He loved her friend and deserved her best self. "I'm glad you're both here. I do hope you'll dance."

"I intend to take her out for the next waltz." Wyndam grinned. "She doesn't have a dance card. They all belong to me."

Claudine laughed. "He can be possessive."

"As I should be," he said in a reverent tone. "You are mine."

"The waltz is the next dance," she told them. Eden tried to ignore her own dance card, but it was like a brand on her wrist. His name was there. Only his name. She hadn't been asked by anyone else; hell, he hadn't even asked her. Would he have if Roslyn hadn't insisted? She didn't think he would have. He had seemed far more interested in Roslyn than Eden. Her heart lurched at that thought. Her night with him had clearly meant more to her than it had to him.

"Wonderful," Lord Wyndam said. "I can't wait to have you in my arms again." He stared at Claudine adoringly, and then he turned his attention to Eden. "Are you going to dance tonight?"

"I hadn't planned to," she admitted.

"Eden doesn't like to dance," Claudine said.

"I don't," she agreed. She was a terrible dancer. "I have had little opportunity to dance. I never had a season." Which she was grateful for most of the time. "My marriage had been arranged."

Wyndam wrinkled his nose. "An archaic practice. I would never do that to one of my children."

"I'm glad we agree on that," Claudine said,

then laughed. "The quadrille is ending. Should we head to the floor?"

Where was the duke? Had he decided he didn't want to dance with her after all? "Go," Eden said. "Have fun. We will talk later."

Claudine nodded as Lord Wyndam led her to the floor. The strands of the waltz were starting, and Eden turned to check with the servants, only to run right into a hard male chest. He wrapped his arms around her to prevent her from falling. "Easy," he said. "I have you."

Hell…it was the duke. His nearness, his scent, brought back so many memories. She almost panicked at the feel of his arms around her again. Eden wanted to be all alone with him and strip off his clothes. His hands, God, she wanted him to touch her everywhere. This was not her lover from that long ago night. He had not been dressed so finely, and he'd been far cruder in his speech to her. "Thank you, Your Grace," she said in a demure tone.

"Were you going somewhere?" he asked. He still had his hands around her waist. Why hadn't he let her go?

"I didn't think you truly wished to dance with me," she told him and pulled back. He didn't let her go far. "I was going to check with the servants."

"You can after our waltz," he told her. "Shall we?" The duke lifted a brow as if telling her she had no choice. She didn't. Not really.

"Yes," she said, her voice wobbled a little as she spoke. Eden had to get herself under control. It wouldn't do for her to fall apart in the middle of the dance floor. That would surely create the scandal that everyone had hoped for.

The duke led her to the floor. He placed one hand at her waist and then the other in her hand. She rested her hand on his shoulder and prayed she didn't embarrass herself in this dance. He didn't speak to her again. They started moving, and she was swirling around the floor with ease, almost as if they did this every day. He led her expertly around the floor, and all the while kept his gaze firmly on hers. It was unnerving.

"Tell me something, Lady Moreland," he demanded. "Do you attend many *ton* functions?"

She panicked for a moment. Had he realized she'd been his lover at Sinbrough's masquerade? "No." Somehow, she'd said that one word without letting her anxiety shine through.

"Is that why you didn't wish to dance with me?"

"It has nothing to do with you, Your Grace." It did have something to do with him. If she had to dance…she both wanted and didn't want it to be him. He was the only one that had any effect on her. "This ball is too important for Roslyn. I want it to be perfect for her."

"But not for you?" He lifted that brow of his again. "You're young enough. Don't you wish to marry someone more suitable?"

"I have no need to tie myself to a man," she said in a bitter tone. "One marriage is enough to cure me of that notion."

He frowned. "You surprise me."

"Is that so terrible?" She smiled. "Not every woman wants to marry, Your Grace, even if you are a duke. You needn't worry about my intentions. I'd never compromise you in the hope of being your duchess." If that were the case, she would already have done so.

"A pity then." His lips quirked into a half smile. "I'd like to see you try."

Was he flirting with her? "Then perhaps I'll surprise you again one day." Eden was unlikely to do that. "But, for now, our dance has come to an end. Enjoy your evening, Your Grace." They came to a stop. Eden curtsied before him. "Thank you for the dance." She turned and left, and didn't glance back at him. Even though she wanted to. Oh, she wanted to. He wasn't hers and never would be. He didn't even know who she was to him, and that was for the best.

If only her heart understood that...

Four

Max tapped his fingers impatiently against the arm of his chair. He hated when he was kept waiting. Didn't they know he was a duke? Duke's were never ignored. Yet that was exactly what was happening to him. It was a novel experience. One he wasn't entirely certain he liked. No. He definitely did not like it. This was beyond ridiculous.

He clenched his mouth into a firm line. If someone didn't join him in the infernal sitting room soon, he'd leave. That would show them. They wouldn't snub him ever again.

And he was starting to sound like a snob. It was a good thing no one could read his mind. Then again, if that were possible, there would be several shocked ladies about town. There were definitely times he had more lascivious thoughts. It might even be amusing to have some of those prudish women privy to some of those desires. Too bad it would be too scandalous or he might actually speak them aloud.

"Your Grace," a female said from behind him. "My apologies for keeping you waiting. Would you like some refreshments? I can ring a servant to bring some."

He swiveled around to meet her gaze. "That is not necessary." He frowned. She was not at all what he had expected. "Are you in charge of this agency?" He lifted a brow. Women didn't...well, *work* wasn't the right word. Many women worked. But they didn't run businesses. At least not to his knowledge.

"I do." She nodded her head as she spoke. "I am Mrs. Banks," she told him. "I opened this agency after my husband's death. It's a long story best left in the past. The gist is that I have a thriving agency that helps employ many women. It is my hope that I will be able to accommodate your needs."

She walked around and sat in the seat opposite of him. She wasn't an elderly widow. In fact, he would even go so far as to say she was attractive and young enough to secure a new husband if she wished. Much like Lady Moreland... Why couldn't he keep that young widow out of his mind? Max held back a groan. She wasn't for him. He didn't want to marry a widow. If he married, and he fully intended to do so in the very near future, he wanted a woman that hadn't already been attached to another man. It was archaic, of course, but he wanted to be the only man that ever touched his wife.

Lady Roslyn was lovely, and she would be perfect for him. She seemed biddable and had the right pedigree. Her only downfall was that scandal her brother had caused. What if she were anything like that rakehell? He knew he shouldn't judge Lady Roslyn by her brother's actions, but he had his niece to consider. It wouldn't do to have a hellion for a wife. What kind of example would that be for Sarah?

Which was what brought him to this meeting... "I need a governess," he told Mrs. Banks. "As I mentioned in my earlier missive to you."

She nodded. "I understand your niece is the

child that one of my ladies will be instructing. May I inquire as to her parents' whereabouts?"

He frowned again. She was being presumptuous. "What does that matter?" The last thing he wished to discuss was his brother and how he had handled the death of his wife. "How does that have anything to do with a governess instructing my niece?"

She sighed. "In order to appoint the right governess for your niece, I need to know what type of child she is and what needs might arise. Some governesses are more suited to certain types of children. Does that make sense?"

He shook his head. "Do they not all teach?" This was becoming more and more irritating. Could a man not simply hire a governess anymore?

Mrs. Banks let out an exasperated breath. "For example," she began, "some children are more unruly and require a strict hand. For them, I have a list of specific governesses that can keep them on task and help them to learn. Others might be emotionally withdrawn, and they will need a lighter touch." She met his gaze and held it firmly. "If I am to assign the right governess, I need more information. So, please tell me about your niece's parents."

She would not let him sidestep the information.

If Sarah didn't need a governess, he would have already told Mrs. Banks to shove it. "They're both dead."

"I see." Did she really see, or was that another platitude? "Both recently?"

She was relentless. "No," he said through gritted teeth. "She never knew her mother." He would not give her any information regarding how Sarah's mother died in childbirth. Let her make her own conclusions. "Her father passed more recently in a riding accident." Damn fool had been bloody foxed and went riding. If he could bring his brother back to life he would. Of course he would only do it to strangle him for leaving him in his current predicament. How could he have left his daughter alone? Then again, he hadn't. His brother would have known Max would take care of Sarah. Hadn't he always done so?

"And you are unmarried?" Mrs. Banks asked.

"Yes," he said in a clipped tone. "But I hope that won't be the case for too long."

"You're seeking a wife." She nodded. "That is good. A governess should never be a replacement for a mother, and it sounds as if your niece has been lacking that role for some time." She folded her hands in her lap. "I think I have the perfect candidate for you. I will see if she is available and send her to your London home in a few days."

"A few days…" He had hoped for someone sooner. "They can't come quicker than that?"

"I'm afraid it isn't possible. She isn't in London currently, and I am not entirely certain she wishes to take on another assignment. I will send word to her immediately, and if she does not wish to take the position, I'll send someone else instead. I do think the lady I have in mind is the perfect candidate, though."

What else could he do? There were no other agencies that came as highly recommended as Banks Vocations. Sarah's education was sorely lacking. One maid at his brother's estate had taken to teaching her, but she was still behind. He didn't want Sarah to feel as if she didn't fit in. Once she was properly educated at home, he could think about sending her to a finishing school. Though that would happen much, much later. She was only eight years old, and he didn't want her so far away yet. It might be different if she'd been born a boy. Then he would be more prepared to send her away to Eton.

"I'll trust your judgement," he said in a curt tone. "Have your candidate come as soon as possible. I expect to know as soon as possible if I should expect someone else. I want to prepare my niece for the arrival of her new governess. Any information you can share with me beforehand will be appreciated." He stared at her. "What is the name of your first choice?"

"I'd rather not say until I know for certain." She pinched her lips together. "You must understand, I take every precaution with those under my wing. I've made mistakes when I opened this agency, and the biggest was giving out names before I was certain. Those ladies were harassed unnecessarily."

"I would never…" How dare she insinuate such a thing? "But I understand your caution." He couldn't risk her ire. This was all for Sarah, and he would keep reminding himself of that until it fully sank in. He would do anything for his niece. Even bite his tongue before Mrs. Banks. "I trust you'll inform me when you're certain, then?"

"Of course," Mrs. Banks said. "I'm always professional." She stood and then gestured for him to follow. "My assistant will have contracts for you to look over and sign. That is nonnegotiable."

She was all business. In another time and place,

he might appreciate that side of her. Though that was not this time or this place. He wanted to be done with this whole situation and return home. He had another society function to attend to later. Would Lady Roslyn be in attendance? If so, then that would mean her chaperone would be as well. Why couldn't he stop thinking about her? And everything had come full circle back to the lovely widow… Max sighed.

She was not for him.

And if he kept telling him that, along with his mantra for Sarah, both might stick. Somehow, he didn't think it would be that easy. He wanted Lady Moreland in his bed, but not as his wife. He couldn't have her and a wife. Which was a pity… Time to sign some contracts and get his niece a governess, and then forget about one very sultry widow.

Tediousness had nothing on societal functions. At least as far as Eden was concerned. They had attended several in as many days, and none stood out. Every single one had been bland, boring, and dare she say it…mundane. It shouldn't bother her. The last thing she wanted to do was gain any attention. She liked blending in and hiding in plain sight. Eden hated socializing and would much rather be at home with a nice book.

Which was why attending the Duke of Sinbrough's masquerade had been so out of character for her. She didn't regret that decision and would happily do it again, or rather…she'd gladly spend the evening in the Duke of Carrington's arms. That didn't mean she would offer herself to him. She just didn't regret her decision to have that one night with him. One night of decadent pleasure was enough. She hoped it was enough… Her mind kept rolling over that night and what he'd made her feel.

Her body heated at the mere thought of the things he'd done with his mouth. Eden had never known it could be like that with a man. Her husband hadn't made her feel that way. She had never enjoyed the marital act. Perhaps that was the difference. Lovers didn't have responsibilities such as securing heirs and estates to maintain. They could enjoy their interludes. She may be wrong, but what if she wasn't? Just another reason to never say vows and tie herself to a union that was destined to fail.

"Isn't this grand?" Roslyn said, exhilaration filling her tone. She had just finished dancing with the Earl of Havenfield. He was not a good choice as a husband, and later she'd tell Roslyn as much. He was a worse reprobate than William had ever been, and to make matters worse, he was also a fortune hunter. She'd heard from a reliable source he'd gambled the last of his income away and was now desperate for a wife to fill his coffers once again. That unfortunate lady would not be Roslyn.

"Quite," she answered in a dry tone. "I'm glad you're finding it entertaining." Eden certainly hadn't. "Have you filled your dance card?"

Roslyn lifted it so Eden could view it. She frowned. The card was indeed filled, and most of those names were not gentlemen she would recommend to her impressionable charge. One stood out more than the others, though. She hadn't realized he was even in attendance. "I see the Duke of Carrington is finally going to have that dance he wanted with you." She wasn't certain how she felt about that development. Was the duke hoping to secure a match with Roslyn? That certainly would make family gatherings a tad uncomfortable.

"Yes," she grinned. "Though he is disappointed

that it isn't a waltz. He arrived too late to have his pick."

"I'm sure he'll manage a quadrille just as well as the waltz." He had been marvelous at the latter. She'd floated in his arms. It made her wonder if there was anything the man was terrible at. "Is there any specific gentleman that has caught your attention?"

Roslyn shook her head. "No." She glanced away at that. Was there a gentleman she wanted to spend more time with? "No one to speak about yet."

Eden narrowed her gaze. "Later, we will discuss some of those men on your dance card. This is not the place, but promise me you won't be alone with any of them. Do not make a decision you will regret later."

Roslyn nodded. "Don't worry," she said in a carefree tone. "I know to be careful." She frowned. "I am already living with my brother's mistakes. I do not need to compound my difficulties with some of my own."

It was a sad fact, but Eden couldn't deny it any more than Roslyn could. They were not outright snubbed, but she couldn't ignore the whispers that many of the *ton* failed to hide. Perhaps they didn't mean to. They gossiped about her and Roslyn whenever they made an appearance. She had been privy to some of the harshest gossip, and she was nearly certain they had meant for her to overhear it.

What is wrong with her, and why did her husband stray?

Is Roslyn as scandalous as her brother?

Will her son grow up to be a reprobate, like his father?

There were so many rumors going around and none of the speculation was favorable. If Roslyn wasn't so determined to marry, Eden would happily stay home for the rest of her days. She didn't need to be a part of society. They had nothing useful to offer her. Hurt was their currency of choice, and it was a price she would not willingly pay.

"It is wise that you recognize that." She nodded toward a gentleman approaching them. He was just as horrid as Lord Havenfield. "I believe your next dance partner is coming to fetch you." At least this dance wasn't a waltz either. The Earl of Coldwater was as frigid as his name implied. He might not be a rake, but he was rumored to be mean…likely the type to beat his wife and children if the mood struck him. "Be careful," she told Roslyn.

"He will not harm me in the middle of the dance floor," Roslyn chided. "You should lighten up a little and dance, too. You don't belong on the edge of the floor watching as everyone else has fun."

"I'm not a young deb," she replied in a soft tone. "I've already been married, became a mother, then a widow. I don't want to repeat any of that." Her life was fine as it was, and she had no desire to make any momentous changes to it.

Roslyn tilted her head to the side. "I hope you change your mind. I wish you happiness. My brother didn't deserve you, but some man out there does. Don't close yourself off when you have so much you could have."

Eden didn't have a chance to respond. Lord Coldwater reached them and held out his arm to Roslyn. She looped her arm through his and allowed him to lead her to the floor. Eden watched the dance and became lost in thought. So lost she hadn't realized when someone came to stand beside her.

"Do you think that is wise?" a man said, startling her back to reality.

She turned toward him and inhaled sharply. How could he possibly become more handsome every time she saw him? "Your Grace," she greeted him. "To what are you referring to?" She lifted a brow.

"Allowing her to dance with Coldwater?" He gestured toward the dance floor. "Or are you not aware of his…proclivities."

Eden frowned. "Should you be speaking with me about such things?" She didn't understand this man. "Are ladies not kept in the dark about things our ears cannot handle?"

He narrowed his gaze and studied her. "Not if she expects to be a proper chaperone to innocents. You may not speak about it, but you should still be aware of it."

"And how would one become aware of something if we do not discuss it?" She tilted her head to the side. "Do gentlemen realize the conundrum they create for ladies when they make dictates such as that one?"

Eden was tired of all the rules men made for women. She wished she didn't have to follow any of them. Unfortunately, she was part of society, and she had to remain a lady in good standing. If she were alone in the world, she might not care, but she had her son, and Roslyn, to consider. For them alone, she held her tongue and kept herself from doing something scandalous. Well, something scandalous she might be caught doing, anyway. It was too late to prevent herself from going to that masquerade and taking a lover. Did he recognize her? She stared up at him and got her answer. If he remembered that night, remembered her, he wouldn't be so nonchalant with her.

His lips quirked. "You amuse me."

She rolled her eyes. "I'm so glad I could be your entertainment for the evening, Your Grace." Eden lifted her hand to her chest and exclaimed, "It's my sole purpose in life to be amusing. Only for you."

He laughed. It was a rich throaty laugh that sent shivers down her spine and tingles in all her lady parts. The duke had laughed with her that night. It was one of the things she'd loved most about it. He'd played with her, gave her pleasure, and made the entire interlude memorable, and yes, enjoyable. Damn him for reminding her. "Your wit and sarcasm are duly noted." He gestured once more to the dance floor. "But I am quite serious. He's not a good man."

"I'm aware," she grudgingly admitted. "And so is Roslyn. But, as she stated before, he claimed his dance. He's not likely to accost her in front of the *ton*. We must keep up appearance." She hated that they skated on the edge of scandal.

"I understand." Maybe he did. Somehow, she

didn't think he fully did, though. "As long as you're aware..."

She lifted a brow. "And what would you have me do? Rush out there and drag her off the floor?" *What a scandal that would make...*

"Of course not," he said. "That's a bit much, don't you think? Just have her refuse future dances with the man."

"If she started refusing all that asked her, she might never dance." Eden shrugged. "As long as she doesn't find herself alone with any of them, she will be all right. You need not worry about her welfare."

He frowned. "Why are you not dancing?"

"I don't enjoy dancing." She wouldn't mind being in his arms again, but she'd never admit that.

"You lie," he said, then leaned down. "I've had you in my arms before. I know exactly what you enjoyed."

Her heart stilled and breathing became more difficult. Was she wrong? Had he actually remembered and now he was calling her out on it? What should she do? "Pardon me?" she squeaked out the words.

"You dance far too beautifully to hate it." He lifted her card and wrote in his name. "I'll prove it to you later. When we waltz again."

With those words, he strolled away. The damage had been done, though. Her heart raced, and she was shaken to the core. Dancing. Of course, he meant dancing. God help her, she wouldn't survive any more interactions with the duke. He drove her mad. With worry and desire….

Five

Avoiding her dance with the Duke of Carrington was high on Eden's list. She nibbled on her bottom lip and considered her options. She couldn't depart the ball. Roslyn had a full dance card, and it would look suspicious if she insisted they leave. They already skated the edges of society because of William's actions. She could not add to the gossip mills just because she feared dancing with the duke again. The last time had left her a mess of emotions and she didn't wish a repeat. She had barely held herself together. The duke was to dance with Roslyn soon, too. Her dance with him was two dances after Roslyn's. If she hoped to avoid him, she would have to be indisposed before the dance with Roslyn ended. He would probably keep a close eye on her after so he could seek her out for their dance.

That dance would not happen…

Eden would do whatever she could to avoid it. She had to… It was imperative to avoid any undue anxiety. Her poor heart could not take any more taxing emotional upheaval.

So, what should she do? She frowned as no obvious answer presented itself. Eden sighed. Why had she allowed her life to become so damned complicated? All she had wanted was one night of pleasure. Just. One. Night. How could she not have foreseen how that selfishness would be her down-fall? If she kept spending any time in the duke's company, he would remember. And if he did… What would he do then? She couldn't predict his reaction, and frankly, didn't wish to attempt it either.

"You look like you're about to either cry or scream," a female said from beside her.

She glanced over and smiled at her friend, Claudine. "I didn't know you were going to attend tonight?"

"It hadn't been the plan." She shrugged. "But there is a widow I need to speak with about becoming a potential member of the league, and, well, sometimes these societal functions are the best places for discreet meetings." She sighed. "I must say part of me wishes that I still avoided society. I don't relish attending balls." She wrinkled her nose. "The price I pay for falling in love with an earl and agreeing to being his wife."

Eden chuckled. "And you'd willingly pay it again." She envied her friend, though she'd never admit that aloud. She had never known love, and definitely not one that appeared to be as deep as what Claudine shared with the Earl of Wyndam. Somehow, she doubted she would ever have anything that profound in her life. It had to be enough that she had her son, and that love was unconditional. He was her world and had been since she first learned she carried him inside of her. That was the only true love she was destined to have in her life, and she was resigned to that fate.

"You're right, of course," Claudine agreed. "I'm lucky to have found love and realize there are many that are not so fortunate." She frowned. "Which is why I am here. Another widow may need my assistance, and I won't fail her."

"I have faith in you," Eden told her. "There is no one more determined than you are. Except perhaps Lady Wyndam. Is she excited about the wedding?" Claudine was marrying the dowager countess's grandson. The older woman had been resigned to the idea of never seeing him wed, but meeting Claudine had changed everything for all of them. It was so lovely to see them all so happy.

"She is," Claudine said. "There are so many plans for it all. My head is swimming. I would be happy to have a simple ceremony, but Lady Wyndam refuses to let such a momentous occasion go by without due celebration."

Of course she did. It was definitely a cause for celebrating. Her grandson was marrying a woman the dowager countess admired. Claudine would be a welcome addition to her family. "When is the wedding?" She hadn't realized how busy she'd become preparing for Roslyn's season. So many days and weeks seemed to have flown by without her notice. "Soon, I'd think?" She frowned.

"In a fortnight," Claudine told her. "You should have an invitation soon. It's going to be at the Wyndam country seat. The countess decided that a proper wedding should have weeks of festivities to celebrate beforehand and there will be a grand house party leading up to the wedding, and for those that wish to stay some more afterward."

"That doesn't leave for much planning…" Roslyn would want to attend. Everyone who was anyone would be at that house party. It was an excellent opportunity for her to meet many eligible gentlemen. They would have to prepare for it and undoubtedly depart London soon. She couldn't recall where the Wyndam country seat was located, but she'd have that information soon enough. They wouldn't expect everyone to arrive on the first day and would allow traveling time for all those invited. She doubted many would stay for the actual wedding. Most would be lured away by the idea of a grand house party though.

Claudine blew out an exasperated breath. "It has not escaped my notice. I've never seen Lady Wyndam so filled with enthusiasm. She's running poor Juliet into exhaustion." Miss Juliet Adams was the countess's companion. She did anything and everything the countess needed.

"Then she'll be glad to see this wedding at an end," Eden laughed. She glanced around. She had been so caught up in her conversation with Claudine, she'd forgotten her need to escape the ballroom. Drat. The duke was currently dancing with Roslyn. She was running out of time and had to soon if she hoped to avoid that dance. "I am looking forward to your wedding. It is sure to be a happy day."

"I hope so," Claudine said. "Ah, I see the lady I need to speak with." She placed her hand on Eden's arm. "I will come for tea soon. We have much to discuss." With that, Claudine left her alone, and Eden took that opportunity to exit the ballroom. She did not know where she was headed, but she knew she had to leave as fast as possible.

MAX LIKED LADY ROSLYN. SHE WAS AMICABLE, lovely, and ideal for the position of his wife. But she didn't spark any genuine emotion in him. When he was near her, he felt…nothing. Was that a good thing? Would it make their possible marriage easier to stomach? He certainly had no real desire to wed. He only entertained the notion now, for Sarah's sake.

"Tell me something, Lady Roslyn," he began. He did not know where he was going with this, but their conversation had been stilted from the moment they began this dance. There were only so many ways to discuss the weather. It rained. The end. "Where has your chaperone gone?" He glanced around the ball-room and couldn't locate her. Had she run scared? Did she dread dancing with him that much? That bothered him more than he wanted to admit. What had he done to make her so skittish? He had to know, and he would, as soon as he located her.

Lady Roslyn glanced around and then shrugged. Not a very ladylike action, but it made her seem more…relatable. "I wish I knew," she told him. Lady Roslyn frowned. "It's not like her to disappear. I hope she's not ill."

"Is that the only reason she might leave?" He lifted a brow. She was running from him. He didn't know how he knew that with such certainty, but he did. He'd bet his entire estate on it. "Should we find her?" He needed to locate her. It made little sense, but he felt it in his bones. He was drawn to her, and he didn't know why.

"After the dance is finished," she told him between turns. "I'll check the ladies' retiring room. If she's ill, that is likely where she'll be."

He nodded. Lady Roslyn could check there. Max had other plans. That was the obvious place for her to hide, but she didn't seem the sort to take the easy path. He'd look elsewhere, and if he was meant to find her, he would. Either way, they would speak again. He'd ensure it.

The music slowed and then came to an end. Max bowed before Lady Roslyn. "Thank you for the dance. Please inform me if you need any assistance locating your chaperone."

"I will, Your Grace." She curtsied, and then rushed off to find Lady Moreland. At least he presumed that was what she went off to do.

Max walked in the opposite direction. Last he noticed, the young widow she'd been deep in a discussion with a different lady. If he was not mistaken, that lady was betrothed to the Earl of Wyndam. How were they acquainted? That was a question for another day or when he found her. He stopped at the location he'd last seen her and glanced around, then grinned. It was near the balcony doors that led out to a terrace. He'd been at this manor house before. That terrace had a staircase that led down to the gardens below. It was such a lovely night for a stroll. Had she gone out there? He was about to find out.

He walked toward the doors and exited the ballroom. The moon was full and bright, giving Max enough illumination to guide him over the balcony and to the nearby staircase. There were several people enjoying the night sky, but when none of them were Eden, he strolled down the stairs. There were not as many people at the edges of the garden as there had been on the terrace. It was far more scandalous to go this far, and even more so deeper into the garden.

The scent of flowers of all sorts drifted toward him. He followed that scent as if it would lead him to his quarry. Maybe it would… He took a path that wound around and stopped at the center of the garden. An intricate fountain lay in the middle with benches encircling it. Eden sat on one of them and leaned over to let her hand drift in the water. She looked so lovely in the moonlight. Almost like the goddess depicted in marble before her, inviting him to join her.

"I do believe this is our dance," he said.

She jerked upright and turned to meet his gaze. Her mouth fell open. He didn't know if it was in shock or if she failed to find the right words. Either way, it was adorable. His lips quirked upward as he waited for her to catch her bearings. He held his hand out to her in invitation. She glanced at it, then back up to his face. "There is no music out here."

"Do we need music?"

She tilted her head to the side. "It usually helps one keep the rhythm of the dance."

"We can make our own," he said. "There are no rules between us. Only what we decide."

Something about this, about her was so familiar. Like she belonged with him… Max couldn't remember feeling like this with another woman. No, that wasn't true. There was another, but Eden wasn't her. He didn't know who she was, but surely he'd recognize her if he found her again.

She shook her head. "Rules exist for a reason."

"Is that so?" He lifted a brow. "Sometimes breaking them is the only thing one can do. Break them with me, Lady Moreland." He wanted desperately to call her Eden, but refrained. That was an intimacy he wanted her to grant him. He wouldn't take what she didn't willingly offer.

She breathed in deeply, then stood. "I'm uncertain about this."

"I am," he told her and stepped closer. "This is a moment in time. One that is ripe with magic. Can't you feel it?" Max didn't do whimsy. Where was this nonsense coming from?

It was her. She did this to him.

He held out his hand to her again. "Come, dance with me, darling."

She inhaled sharply. He held his breath. Would she come to him? Slowly, she moved forward until she was within his reach. She only had to take one more step and he could pull her closer. He silently pleaded with her until she took that last step and placed her hand in his. "Lead the way, Your Grace."

He smiled down at her and then brought her closer. Much closer than the waltz would have allowed. They would dance, but he wanted to feel her as they moved. Almost like a much more intimate dance, and one where they wouldn't have clothes between them. They danced in silence. Almost as if they had agreed that speaking would break the spell that had woven around them. Max wanted to kiss her, but held back. He'd already pushed her farther than she seemed willing to go. He'd believed he'd wanted Lady Roslyn, but now he reconsidered. Perhaps a widow was exactly what he needed.

No. That wasn't quite true. *She* was what he *wanted*... And he always got what he wanted. Eden would be *his*. He just needed to convince her that she wanted him as much as he desired her.

Six

Eden leaned against the side of the carriage and stared out the window. There wasn't much to see outside, but it was somehow soothing to watch the trees pass by in a small whir of greens and browns. She kept playing that dance through her mind on repeat. He'd been so charming and wonderful. For a few moments, she had been tempted to tell him everything. He clearly didn't recognize her. What would he do or say if he realized they had an intimate past? She wasn't sure she wanted an answer to that question. The very idea of spilling her secret was not worth considering. It would not lead her down the path she hoped it would.

"What has you so preoccupied?" Roslyn asked.

"You must be thrilled to attend this house party. Just think, in a fortnight, Claudine will be a countess."

"That isn't what is important to her," Eden answered. She'd purposely ignored Roslyn's question. She didn't want to tell her sister-in-law about what had been on her mind the entire journey. "We should be arriving at Wyndam Castle soon." At least she hoped so. She was tired of being in the carriage with too much time to think. Eden needed something else to occupy her mind with. "Are you excited for this house party?"

Roslyn wrinkled her nose. "I am, and I'm not at the same time." She sighed. "I've not had much luck so far this season. I've danced, but none of the gentlemen want me. At least not as their wife."

Eden sat up straighter and stared at her. "What do you mean? Has anyone been inappropriate with you?" She'd ensure none of them came near Roslyn again. "Tell me everything." Her tone was hard as she spoke. She would not tolerate anyone taking advantage of Roslyn.

"No," Roslyn said, then sighed again. "They haven't done or said anything to me." She nibbled on her bottom lip. "I've no cause to lie at your feet. It is the ladies that are gossiping about me, and in turn, it is leading to the gentlemen's ears."

Eden closed her eyes and took a deep breath. This shouldn't surprise her at all. They were all talking about what her foolish husband had done. It didn't matter that he'd paid a dear price for his actions—his life. That wasn't enough for the ladies of the *ton*. They had to malign Eden and Roslyn as well. Blast them all to hell… "Have you heard them gossiping about you?"

"Yes," Roslyn admitted. "None of it has been favorable."

"It'll be different at Wyndam Castle," she said vehemently. Eden would ensure it and enlist Claudine in helping as well. "They wouldn't dare speak ill of you at our friend's home." If they did, they would be asked to leave. She would bet everything on that fact. Claudine had no patience for idiocy.

"I hope so," Roslyn said. "But I do expect the gossipmongers will gladly spread tales about me given the first opportunity. They won't always be around our hostess, will they? Some might speak in ill terms in the privacy of their assigned bedchambers. We cannot control everyone's tongue."

"You're correct, of course," Eden conceded. "But we can curb it as much as possible." She closed her eyes and took a deep breath. A few moments ago, she had wished for something else to occupy her mind with. She should have been careful of what she'd hoped for. This was a problem she should have foreseen. It was equally as compelling as her fascination with the Duke of Carrington…

"Either way, we must forge ahead. There is a gentleman out there who will look past your brother's actions. You didn't even know what he was doing and shouldn't be held to the same light as him. It's ridiculous that the *ton* would even consider you unworthy of society because of his foolishness." Sometimes Eden hated her deceased husband. She'd never say that aloud, though. She had no desire to be judged for her anger. Justified or not…

"It is ridiculous," Roslyn conceded. "But there is no changing any of it. You're right. We must do our best to move forward with our lives." She placed a hand on Eden's arm. "It is all right for you to do the same. You do know that, right?"

"Move forward?" She glanced over to meet Roslyn's gaze. "I like to think I do that every day." She had done some things she never would have considered before. Like having a one-night affair with a certain duke…

"Not just that." Roslyn tilted her head to the

side. "I mean, find a gentleman you could love... Consider marrying again."

Eden shook her head. "I don't wish for that. One marriage was enough for me." She didn't know if she could ever trust a man with her life again. If she wed, she'd become that man's property and have no say in her life. It wasn't just a matter of love. She didn't know what love actually felt like. Eden hadn't loved her husband. It had been an arranged marriage. Trust was the actual issue, no matter how she looked at it. She couldn't imagine allowing herself to have that kind of faith ever again.

"That's sad," Roslyn told her, "and depressing. I know you didn't have a grand love match with my brother. Don't you think it is time to have that?" She held up her hand when Eden started to speak. "No, let me say my piece. You don't have to marry again. If you can't find it in yourself to trust a man again; I understand that. But love... It's an unfamiliar emotion. Find a man you can give your heart to and have a grand affair. One that you can look back on for many years with fondness—that doesn't require you to say any vows before a man of God. You're a widow and have more freedom. Use that to your advantage."

Hadn't she already done that? She didn't love the duke, but she had one night in his arms. One night he didn't remember…or rather didn't recall it was her. He might not have any issues remembering the actual night, just the woman he spent it with. She had to admit it bothered her a little that he didn't seem to have any memory of her. "I'll consider it," she said in a quiet tone. "That's all I can promise."

"Good," Roslyn said. "I want you to have happiness."

"You deserve that too," Eden told her. She turned to glance out the window again. What did true happiness feel like? There was so much she didn't have in her life. Roslyn was right. She should know more about love before she tossed the idea of it aside. "Look," she said as she gestured out the window. "The castle is just over that hill." *Thank heavens…* She wanted out of the bloody carriage and away from Roslyn's prying gaze.

MAX DIDN'T THINK HE WOULD EVER MAKE IT TO Wyndam Castle. He hated extended carriage rides. He wished he'd had the foresight to ride instead of traveling in his carriage, but that wouldn't have been prudent. His stay at Wyndam Castle would be lengthy, and he'd need his trunks. Yes, he could have sent them in the carriage without him, but he hadn't thought of that. No going back now, regardless. He was on his path, and he had traveling companions with him.

"Glaring out the window will not make the carriage go any faster," Crawford drawled. "In fact, I'd wager it will make the journey even more unbearable." Max would not take his irritation out on his friend. Though it sounded like an excellent notion when the marquess was being a right arse.

"I am not glaring at anything," he said in a petulant tone. He sounded like a spoiled child. *Hell.* They had to get to the damn castle soon.

"Of course not," Lyonsdale said, then barely suppressed a laugh. Max was not stupid. The earl was amused with him. Maybe he could take his irritation out on the two of them. They didn't seem to care that they were making his mood darker by the second. "You're aglow with joy. It's clear to anyone that takes a moment to glance upon your fair visage."

Max turned to face the earl and nearly growled, "Be careful or it will be your fair visage that glows…" He paused briefly, then added, "Red, mixed with a little blue and purple. You know, after my fists bounce off it a few times."

"You are in a mood," Crawford said in a low tone. "Why?"

He understood their confusion. Max had been unable to control his frustration for days. Ever since his dance with a certain countess at that last ball he'd attended. He needed to see her again. She was the only reason he had decided to attend this house party. He knew she would be there. Her friendship with the bride, and her role as a chaperone, would dictate that. If not for his need for her, he'd have stayed home. Max hated that he'd be away from Sarah for so long. At least he now had a governess settled in with her. She would be well taken care of by his servants, the nanny, and the governess. "I'll be fine once we're able to depart from this carriage…" When he could lay his gaze upon the woman that was haunting his dreams. "…and not have to get back inside for days."

"I can understand your need to stretch your legs," Lyonsdale responded. "We shouldn't be confined to the carriage much longer. It's been a while since I've been this far outside of London myself. I don't particularly like visiting my family estate."

"Touché," Crawford said. "We all have our crosses to bear." He sighed. "Is that all it is?" He met Max's gaze. "You're feeling some pent-up frustration after being confined here with us?" He leaned forward. "Or is there something more pressing brewing here?"

"Such as?" Max lifted a brow. They couldn't know he was nearly obsessed with a young widow. No one knew. He hadn't said one word to anyone, and if he had, these two would have been top on his list to unburden himself.

"It's been rumored you're in search of a wife," Lyonsdale said. The words were like a dinner bell going off in the silence. No one spoke for several seconds, as if they were waiting for Max to erupt with madness. They would wait for a long time for that to happen. He wouldn't give them any reason to think he'd lost his mind. At least no more than usual…

"I am," he said in a calm tone. "That should not surprise either of you. I have different responsibilities now."

"Sarah," Crawford said. There was nothing else to add. "You think she needs a mother, then?"

"You don't?" Max tilted his head to the side. "She's had enough grief in her young life. I don't want her to feel any other burdens." And he didn't know what kind of father type he'd be for her. She needed someone that she could always be depended on. He wanted to believe he could be that person for her, but on the chance he couldn't... Max needed a wife.

"I admire you and your fortitude," Lyonsdale began. "But I don't envy you. We are here for you." He nodded at Crawford. "It's why we decided to attend this house party. Though we do consider Wyndam a friend, it's you we're really enduring this possible parson's trap for."

"You're all heart," Max said drolly. "Whatever would I do without friends like you?"

"It's true," Crawford said. "You're lucky to have us."

Max rolled his eyes. "*Soooo* fortunate." Why were they not at Wyndam Castle yet? This trip was going to be his undoing. He prayed it would be worth all the trouble in the end. If it concluded with a certain widow in his arms, and his life, it might just live up to his expectations. He blew out a breath. "I appreciate what you're willing to do for me." Max grinned. "Even potentially, as you stated, finding a bride of your own."

"Blasphemy," Lyonsdale said.

"Are you trying to curse us?" Crawford added. "That's rude."

Max laughed for the first time since they had started their journey to Wyndam Castle. Perhaps this would not be so terrible after all. He grinned, then said. "I don't know. Why wouldn't I wish happiness for my two closest friends?"

They glared at him in response. Max ignored them and whistled happily as he stared out the window once again.

Seven

Eden hadn't slept well the evening before. She had tossed and turned the entire night, plagued by wanton dreams of a certain duke. She'd woken with sweat slicked skin and an aching throughout her entire body. The need that had coursed through her had been unshakeable. After her failure to fall back asleep, she'd given up and crawled out of her bed to start her day. The sun hadn't even risen yet and darkness had enveloped her assigned bedchamber. She wished she could erase the visions that filled her mind. If only she hadn't had that one night with him. Maybe then she could forget about him. Wishing for something didn't make it so, though.

Somehow, she would have to find a way to move past her fascination with the man.

Maybe she should find something to read. The servants were just going about their day and breakfast wouldn't be ready for at least another hour. Claudine had explained that it would be served buffet style so everyone could eat as they awakened. They didn't want a rigid morning schedule. That was understandable, with so many guests expected for the house party. They were going all out to celebrate the upcoming wedding.

She sighed and decided to leave her bedchamber. Even if she didn't find a book to read, she could always take a walk in the gardens. It might be a little brisk so early in the morning, but it might help clear her mind. With her decision made, she headed down the stairs and then toward the library. She could even take a book into the garden. It sounded like a pleasant way to pass the time. At least until she was no longer the only one awake and prepared to start the day…

She slid into the library and frowned. The sun had started to rise, but it was still too dark to browse. She found a nearby candelabrum and lit the candles within it, then carried it with her to the shelves. She slid her fingers over the spines until a dark red one caught her attention. Eden slid it out and flipped it open. She smiled when she read the title: *A Lady's Guide to Finding a Lover*. Should she read it? What did she have to lose? If anything, it might prove entertaining. There was no author listed. Perhaps a real lady had penned the guidebook.

She blew out the candles and set the candelabrum down, then went to the doors on the other side of the library. They led out into the garden, and she could go out there. After she walked a little, the sun should be bright enough for her to read. It would give her time to find the perfect spot to become lost in her book. Eden was tired, but she also felt invigorated.

She reached a spot in the gardens that she found to be gorgeous. On one side, roses of red, pink, and white bloomed. On the other side, various shades of purple and yellow roses had been planted. It was almost like a rainbow of colors that filled her senses. She closed her eyes and took a deep breath. Yes, this was the perfect location for her to relax and read. Eden sat on a nearby stone bench and settled in to read the book. She flipped it open and read the title of the first section of the book: *How to Select the Perfect Lover*.

Her lips twitched. How did one know a man

could be the perfect lover? That seemed an impossibility... Just looking at a man wouldn't give a woman all the information she needed to make such a decision. Not to mention that the term *perfect* was a lofty goal to undertake.

She started reading the passage and realized that she'd been right. Perfect was in the eye of the beholder, so to speak. What worked for one person might not for another. It wasn't so much as finding a perfect lover, but one that was perfect for her. It was up to the individual to decide what they wanted most. An intriguing concept, and perhaps one she could have used all those weeks ago when she had chosen the Duke of Carrington. Not that she thought she'd made a terrible decision. On the contrary, she had been fortunate in having chosen him.

Eden wouldn't change that night for anything. In fact, if she had one complaint, it would be that one night hadn't been nearly long enough. She wanted to have several nights. Perhaps weeks or even months... That was the true impossibility. To have that length of time might lead to consequences she couldn't live with. Consequences that should only exist within the benefits of marriage... She couldn't afford to take those kinds of risks. She had to think of her son and what society might do if she found herself in a predicament that wouldn't go unnoticed.

The book gave her much to consider. She wanted to read it all, but perhaps not now. Soon, others would be around, and she didn't want to read it when someone might notice and ask questions.

"That must be an interesting book," a gentleman said.

Eden closed her eyes and barely suppressed a groan. Of course it would be him. The one person she had hoped to avoid, and he'd caught her reading a book that only made her think of him more. "I suppose it is that." She kept her tone as neutral as she could manage. Eden glanced up and met his gaze. What else could she say to him? She'd never felt so utterly incompetent before. The mere act of conversing with him seemed too difficult. She smiled at him, but didn't feel it. "I thought I would go see about breakfast. If you'll pardon me." She stood.

He reached out and placed his hand on hers. "Wait."

She took a slow breath and met his gaze once again. It seared her to her bones. "Yes?"

"I'll escort you." He smiled at her. "You can tell me about your book." He gestured toward the little red tome.

Drat. How was she going to avoid that conversation? "It's not that interesting," she said. "But you may escort me to breakfast. You can tell me which of the activities the Dowager Countess has planned for us that you're anticipating the most." Eden prayed it was enough of a diversion for him to forget about her book.

"As long as I'm in your company," he said in a droll tone. "All of them sound appealing." His lips twitched. "And perhaps you will still deign to tell me about that uninteresting book of yours."

So far, everything was not going the way she wanted. Eden prayed it that changed. She glared at him, but held her tongue. Replying to that comment would only bait him further, and that was the last thing she wanted.

MAX COULDN'T BELIEVE HIS LUCK. HE'D BEEN unable to sleep and left his room in search of something, anything, to occupy his mind with. When he'd wandered into the garden, he hadn't thought he'd find the very reason he'd been tossing and turning awaiting him there. Perhaps he should quit questioning fate and accept what it had in store for him. That sentiment seemed a bit trite, but he couldn't shake the feeling he was exactly where he should be, and this woman was his future.

"Do you wish to walk a little before we go inside?" He wasn't ready to share her with anyone else yet. If he could keep her in the garden a little while longer, he would, but he'd never force her to remain where she did not wish to. He could only pray she wanted to be with him as much as he desired it.

She jolted her gaze toward his and nibbled on her bottom lip in contemplation. After a few agonizing moments, she nodded. "It's a lovely morning. I wouldn't mind remaining out here for now."

Max barely held back a grin. "You enjoy being in the garden?"

"I don't have a garden nearly this lovely in London," she admitted. "But I love flowers and all the scents that surround me. If I return to the country, I'll have to do more about the gardens there. They never held my interest before…" Her voice trailed off and she stared at the roses nearby.

"Before?" he prompted. He had an idea of what she had been about to say, but he didn't want to be presumptive.

She was quiet, still contemplative. He didn't think she was going to answer him, and he wasn't certain how he felt about that. Max wanted to understand her, but she seemed more inclined to keep distance between them. Of course, it was far more likely he was letting his own uncertainties rule his thoughts. She stopped and ran her fingertips over one of the roses, then began to speak. "My husband didn't allow me to make many changes on the estate. He believed things like gardens should be left to those that understood them far more than a woman with little education."

Max frowned. "I didn't realize that much went into gardening."

She smiled. "Understanding plants and how they grow does help them bloom properly." She sighed. "I'm no expert, but I have read a few books about it. I had hoped to convince my husband to let me try." Eden nibbled on her lip. "But then, as he was wont to do, he acted recklessly, and that had led to his death, and in turn, my freedom."

He didn't know what to say to that. The former Earl of Moreland had been an idiot. He'd had a treasure and treated her as if she were nothing. Max would never have done that. "And what are you doing with your freedom?"

It hurt to ask her that. What if it meant he had no chance at winning her heart? Her marriage hadn't been a good one. Why would a widow, one that wanted for nothing, risk marriage again? What did he have to offer her that she would want to take a chance on him? His title? There were some women that would readily agree to be his duchess. Eden didn't seem like she cared to rise in ranks.

She shrugged. "Nothing extraordinary," she told him. "It's enough that the choices are my own, and I don't have to answer to anyone."

He nodded. "Something most men take for granted."

Eden stared up at him, the surprise in her eyes evident. "Most men wouldn't admit they have more say in their lives than women."

Max wasn't a stupid man. He had understood what she hadn't been saying in their conversation. She'd felt suffocated in her marriage. Her opinions had been swept aside as nothing, and her true desires even less than that. Her husband hadn't respected her. "I'd like to think I'm more progressive than those men you are throwing me in with."

Her lips twitched. "Admittedly," she began. "You do appear to be more agreeable to converse with." They turned onto another path. This one led them back toward the manor. "But I also am not that acquainted with you. I'm certain there is much I do not know about you."

"True," he agreed. "But we can rectify that." Max smiled down at her. "If you're willing." *Please let her be willing...*

She was silent again. It always made him anxious when she didn't reply straightaway. Eden drew in a breath. Almost as if she was taking a fortifying burst of air into her. "I'd like that." Her tone was so soft, so quiet, he almost didn't hear her words.

"You would?" he replied before he had time to consider the words leaving his mouth.

"You sound surprised." She tilted her head to the side and studied him. "Why?"

"You seem...." He struggled for the right words. "Private."

"I am," she agreed. "But, sometimes, I have to take a chance. If I don't, I won't truly be free." Eden smiled. "And we have more than a fortnight here in the country. Why not use that time to our advantage?"

"I couldn't agree more," he told her. First task completed. He had a whole list of items he needed to check off, and so far, everything was working out in his favor. They reached the house, and he opened the door for her. Time to break their fast, but later he would find her again. The more time he spent in her company, the bigger the chance he'd convince her to be his duchess.

Eight

Eden kept replaying her conversation with the Duke of Carrington earlier that morning. He'd almost seemed…different. Normally there was an arrogance drifting off him waves. She hadn't seen that in the garden. What could have changed in him? Perhaps she'd read him wrong in their previous encounters. *No.* His arrogance was still a part of him. He had just held it in check for some reason.

She regretted nothing that had happened between them. That didn't mean she was ready to remind him they were already intimately aware of each other. Besides, she did want to become more acquainted with him. It would help her make a decision about him. If she thought they might have more between them, then she'd tell him the truth. Otherwise, there was no reason to admit they'd had a night of passion. A night so erotic she hadn't been able to forget about it. Perhaps that was why he was drawn to her now. Did he know who she was? No. She didn't think he did. He'd have said something if he had recognized her. Wouldn't he? She hadn't exactly been forthcoming why would he be? She would like to believe he wouldn't pretend with her, but she did not know one way or the other without asking him. Something she didn't want to do.

"I am considering wearing my green gown to dinner tonight," Roslyn said. She stared at the gowns that had been prepared for her by her lady's maid, Alice. She nibbled on her bottom lip. "What do you think?"

"The green is lovely," Eden told her. "But more importantly, you'll look lovely in any of your gowns. Wear what will make you happy." Eden certainly intended to do that herself.

Roslyn nodded. "I'll definitely wear the green one." She walked over to and rang for the maid. They were sharing a dressing room that joined their bedchambers together. There were several guests, and most had to share rooms. Since Roslyn and Eden were close friends of Claudine's, they were in the family quarters. It was far more peaceful, and they didn't have to suffer any unwanted attention.

"What is bothering you?" Eden asked her. She'd been in a downhearted mood since she'd joined her to dress for dinner. Roslyn was her main priority and if something was bothering her, she needed to know what it was.

Roslyn blew out a breath. "Some of the ladies…" She glanced away from Eden. "Haven't been the most pleasant."

They hadn't been at Wyndam Castle for very long and were already gossiping? Who was she kidding? Of course they were. That was what some of the more devious members of the *ton* did. They lived for gossip, and the more salacious the better. "Are they being rude to you?"

"Not directly," she admitted. "I've overheard some unpleasantness." She still hadn't met Eden's gaze.

"What are they saying?" Eden needed to know it all. "Is it about me?"

Roslyn glanced toward the door as if she were willing Alice to come through it and stop their conversation. It didn't matter if the maid did come in, Eden wasn't letting the topic drop. "Tell me," she ordered.

"All right," Roslyn said in a resigned tone. "But you're not going to like it."

"No one ever likes the things they overhear about themselves." They had been talking about her since her foolish husband had gotten himself killed. "I refuse to let anyone control me or my emotions. But I cannot battle what I don't have all the information on."

"It wasn't about you," Roslyn said. "At least not directly." She slumped down into a chair and stared at the floor. "It all comes back to him."

Ah... William. The gift his death left them was one that kept giving, and none of it had been or probably would be good. "I wish he had thought about what his actions would do," Roslyn said, then sighed. "Unfortunately, he never considered anyone other than himself." Her husband had been a selfish fool.

"My marriage prospects are not good." She played with her skirts as she spoke. "And that is all they seem to be able to discuss. As if my difficulties give them a particular bit of joy."

Eden clenched her fingers into her palm. Her nails bit into her flesh and she used that pain to hold her anger in check. She didn't want to take out her rage on Roslyn. It wasn't her fault, and the person who had led them down this path couldn't rectify any of it. "I'm sorry," she said in a quiet tone. "If I could change any of it, I would."

Roslyn's smile wobbled. She clearly fought tears, and it broke Eden's heart. "You're a wonderful sister." She closed her eyes and took a deep breath. "It's too bad I couldn't have had a brother that deserved to have you for his wife."

"Some things cannot be foreseen," she told her. That was a lesson she had learned in the hardest of ways. If she could prevent Roslyn from experiencing even a tiny bit of that pain, she would. She couldn't regret the path she had taken, if not for her marriage she wouldn't have her son. But discovering the strength of her fortitude hadn't been easy. "Life isn't always fair. But what we do with the difficulties life has in store for us shows the world who we really are. What do you want everyone to see in you?"

"That they can't destroy me with their viciousness." She held her chin up. "I will not break down and be what they want me to be. I won't give up, and I refuse to believe that I'll never find love."

Eden smiled. "Good." She leaned down and kissed Roslyn's cheek. "Hold on to that strength. If you want love, then you shall have it. There is a gentleman out there that will recognize it and is smart enough to be the man you need him to be."

"I hope so," Roslyn said.

The door opened and Alice stepped in. "Are you ready to dress for dinner?"

"We are," Eden said. "Start with Roslyn."

Eden hadn't decided what she would wear, but her gown wasn't nearly as important as Roslyn's. She did want to look her best, though. The duke would be there, and she wanted him to like what he saw when his gaze landed on her. It was time for her to keep her head held high and borrow some of the strength Roslyn had inside of her. She wouldn't have been nearly as brave at Roslyn's age. If she had, then she wouldn't have ever married the Earl of Moreland, and perhaps she might have found a modicum of happiness.

MAX SAT IN THE EARL OF WYNDAM'S STUDY AND stared at his friends. Wyndam's wedding was soon, and the man had never looked as happy as he did at the prospect of having a wife. Nothing was ever as simple as it seemed. How had the man known he was in love? Max didn't think he was capable of such an emotion. With Eden… He might be able to love her. If there was ever a woman he could love, it would be her.

"My mother is sending Portia here," the Marquess of Crawford said in an irritated tone. "She said I can be her chaperone and didn't want to hear any arguments about the matter."

Lyonsdale lifted a brow. "How does your sister feel about that?"

Lady Portia North was Crawford's younger sister. She had launched three seasons ago but had been a veritable wallflower. It was driving Crawford's mother mad. The duchess feared her only daughter would become a spinster. The duke didn't seem to care either way. Portia would never want for anything. The duke had ensured she would always have enough funds to see to all of her needs. The money alone should attract a suitor, but the duke refused to give his daughter to a fortune hunter just to avoid her becoming a spinster. Crawford, being the heir to a dukedom, was sought after as much as Carrington. Which is how they'd become such good friends so many years ago. They had bonded over their titles and the hassle that came with them.

"I don't know what Portia is thinking," Crawford sighed. "She hates being in society, but she promised mother she would try one more season." He scrubbed his hands over his face and sighed. "But if she doesn't find a gentleman to marry by the end, she refuses to go through it all again. I think she *wants* to be a spinster."

That was odd... "Don't all women want to marry?" Max lifted a brow. After he spoke the words, he realized it made him sound like an arse. Eden wouldn't want to marry again. But she'd already had a husband and knew it wasn't always what a bride envisioned it would be.

"Portia certainly doesn't." Crawford frowned. "I think if she does marry, her future husband will have to be some sort of paragon."

Lyonsdale frowned. "What is she even looking for?"

"I wouldn't presume to know," Crawford admitted. "And it is a conversation I don't wish to have with my sister."

Lyonsdale stared at the marquess as if he had grown two heads. "Portia is a lovely lady. She should have found someone to love by now."

What an odd statement for the earl to have made... Lyonsdale was closer to Crawford than Max was. He'd spent a lot of time during school breaks with Crawford and his family. Did he know Portia better than her brother did? If he didn't have his own issues, he'd ask Lyonsdale more questions. Perhaps he had feelings for Lady Portia North. If that were so, how would Crawford feel about his sister and his friend being together?

"Love isn't something you can plan," Wyndam said. "I certainly hadn't been looking for it when Claudine came into my life. If Lady Portia wishes to fall in love first, that cannot be forced. It'll happen when it is meant to."

Crawford laughed. "Perhaps she has already found love, but the gentleman of her dreams is too stupid to love her in return."

Lyonsdale glanced away at the marquess's statement. Perhaps Crawford saw more than Max had originally thought. If the earl did love Lady Portia North, why was he not courting her? Did he think she wouldn't have him? He supposed anything was possible. However, none of that was his concern. He had his own countess to contend with, and he had plans to win her heart.

"Are you excited for the wedding?" Maxw asked Wyndam. They were supposed to go to the drawing room soon, and then escort the ladies to dinner. This was a time for solitude and camaraderie.

"I'm more excited for the marriage than the wedding." Wyndam grinned. "I'm ready to have Claudine as my wife. The wedding is more of a necessary evil."

Max nodded. He could see how the earl would feel that way. He would look upon his wedding in much the same way. "Your grandmother is enjoying all of this." The dowager countess was why they were having such a long house party before the wedding.

"And that is why I agreed to all of this." He sipped on a glass of brandy. "I'd have married Claudine by special license and have been done with it. Grandmother wouldn't hear of such a plan. She wanted us to have a proper wedding and celebration."

If he could get Eden to agree to marry him, he'd have to be stealthier than the earl had been. Perhaps he'd abscond with her to Scotland and elope. That would be preferable to all these shenanigans. "I admire your fortitude." Maxw grinned.

"Are you mocking me?" Wyndam lifted his brows.

Max held up his thumb and forefinger and held them apart slightly and said, "Only a little."

Crawford laughed then. "We're happy for you, but none of us envy you."

Max wouldn't go that far. He wanted a wife. He wanted Eden. The wedding festivities though… He'd gladly skip that part, and as Wyndam had stated, go straight to the marriage part.

"You say that now," Wyndam said. "But one day you will find a woman cannot live without and understand my anxiousness. When that happens, I'll be here, and maybe I'll even offer some sage advice." He took another sip of his brandy. "But more likely I'll remind you of this day and laugh."

The wicked grin on the earl's face made Max chuckle. He had great friends and a good life. Soon, hopefully, he'd have the wife he desired too.

Nine

Max stared across the back lawn at Wyndam Castle and frowned. The activities that had been planned for the weeks leading up to the wedding were meant to entertain the guests. He supposed most might find them so, but he had one purpose for being there. To woo a certain widow, and some of those activities only proved to make that goal less unattainable. She was always surrounded by other individuals and made it more difficult to have some quality time alone with her.

Today's undertakings would include outdoor archery, a hunt some of the men wished to participate in, and a picnic. Servants were already setting up tents and tables for the picnic later that afternoon, and many of the guests were gathering around the archery area. He scanned the guests, looking for her. His lips curved upward when his gaze landed on her. She stood next to her sister-in-law, Lady Roslyn Barrett and Lady Portia North, the Marquess of Crawford's sister. Crawford had mentioned Portia was going to attend. A fact he hadn't been pleased about. Where was the marquess? Shouldn't he be more aware of his sister's activities?

Since Portia wasn't his concern, he didn't bother to find the marquess. If Crawford wasn't worried, then he would not be either. He set a pace toward Eden though. Since he hoped to win her hand, he'd have to spend some time with her to accomplish that feat. Was she going to participate in the archery? He would if she decided to as well. It would give them something to do together. He hadn't been able to talk with her since their time in the garden several days ago. Every time he got close, she found a reason to flee, almost as if she was afraid to be alone with him. Why? He had to know what she'd been thinking. The last thing he wanted to do was have her fear him.

He reached the ladies and bowed slightly. "Good morning," he greeted them.

Lady Portia met his gaze and smiled. "Your Grace," she greeted. "Are you going to participate? I'd have thought you would be more interested in the hunt. My brother certainly is."

Max's lips twitched. "Some hunts are more tedious than others. I can see why this one would appeal more to Crawford. Archery has more appeal for me." He turned his attention to Eden. "Are you going to participate?"

"I had been considering it," she said, then nibbled on her bottom lip. He wanted to lean over and suck on that very lip and ease any pain her teeth had left in their wake, and then he wanted to kiss her until their breaths mingled until they shared a breath in unison. Her cheeks pinkened at his perusal. "I think they're having some sort of partnership or teams planned."

"Is that so?" He glanced around them. Max could use this to his advantage. He just had to know how. The dowager countess was talking to the housekeeper. That was where he would get his answers. "Pardon me while I go discover what the plan is for the day."

He strode over to them and waited for the dowager countess to acknowledge him. "Lady Wyndam," he greeted her. Then glanced at her companion and frowned. He'd been wrong. It wasn't the housekeeper, but her companion she'd been talking to. What was her name again?

He must have stared at her for far too long because she lifted a brow, then said, "Miss Juliet Adams." He felt like an arse. "Your Grace." Her tone was biting as she spoke. It was filled with disapproval he felt in his bones. What had he done to her? Certainly forgetting her name didn't warrant such contempt.

He nodded. "Miss Adams." He kept his tone neutral. Whatever issues Miss Adams had with him, he didn't wish to harbor any of out at that moment. "Can you tell me what the plans are for archery this morning?"

"You don't wish to join the hunt?" Lady Wyndam lifted a brow. "I would have thought you'd wish to go with the rest of your cohorts."

Max grinned. All of his friends must have decided to join the hunt. He wouldn't have gone even if he had other motives for his actions. "I've never been fond of hunting." Though it would have been nice if at least one of his friends had stayed behind.

At that moment, another gentleman came to stand beside him. "No worries," he said. "Not all of us have decided to run off to the hunt. I lost and stayed behind. We all know how you abhor hunting." There were reasons for that. Reasons he never talked about unless he had to.

Max nodded at his friend, the Earl of Lyonsdale. "Where is Crawford?"

"He was going to join the hunt as well," he said, then glanced toward Lady Portia. "But he begrudgingly admitted that he should not abandon his sister."

"Oh?" Max lifted a brow. "She was under the assumption he plans to do just that."

Lyonsdale nodded. "He still refuses to participate in archery, but he's nearby."

He was probably lurking in some nearby bushes with a lady with loose morals. Crawford was one of the biggest rakes in the *ton*. He turned back to Miss Adams and Lady Wyndam. "About the archery then…"

Miss Adams grinned. "We'll it is good that you are both here then. We are short of male partners for the ladies and feared we would have to double some of the women up, and well, that's not fair, is it?"

"Partners?" He frowned. He hadn't paid close attention and must have missed that.

"It's a competition, but with a twist." She grinned. "We thought we would make it more interesting. The women will pair up with the men, then compete against their partner. Whoever wins gets a boon."

He narrowed his gaze. "What kind of boon?"

"Whatever the lady," she said, then coughed, "or, well, the man wishes from the loser. However, I must state it cannot be something that would be compromising. We're not trying to force anyone into an unwanted marriage. This is all supposed to be fun."

Max grinned, then turned to Lyonsdale. "Go fetch the marquess. He's going to participate."

Lyonsdale lifted a brow. "Is he?"

"Yes," Max said in a firm tone. "Then drag him over to his sister's side. We're going to form a partnership with those ladies."

He nodded at Miss Adams and Lady Wyndam, then strode back over to Eden's side. This was the best idea they had come up for them during this house party, and he fully intended to win. He had a boon in mind for Eden, and he wanted to claim it as soon as possible.

EDEN STARED AT THE BOW IN HER HAND. SHE HAD never particularly liked archery. She was a passable shot, but she'd never fully enjoyed the sport. Now she was going to participate in the game. Not because she wanted to. Not even because Roslyn wanted her to. No, she was going to nock her bow and take aim for one reason only. She'd been charmed into it by one Duke of Carrington.

They were doubled up, but in sets of three. She was shooting with the duke, Roslyn was with the Marquess of Crawford, and Lady Portia, the marquess's sister, was with the Earl of Lyonsdale. They all gathered near their prospective targets. Eden was shooting first. She'd volunteered so she could get her shots off and be done. At least until the next round… She nocked her arrow on the bow and took a deep breath and raised it to aim at the target. After a few steadying breaths, she let the arrow loose. It flew toward the stacks of hay and landed a little below the mark. Not her best. If she had any hope of not owing the duke a boon, she'd have to do better.

"Not bad," the duke said. She turned toward him and noticed the grin he couldn't hide. Somehow, she doubted he wanted to either.

She narrowed her gaze. "I suppose you think you can do better?"

He shrugged. "Love," he began. "Archery is not what I'm good at." Then he leaned a little closer until his heat enveloped her. His tone was husky as he spoke. "If you want, I can show you exactly where my talents lie."

Eden closed her eyes and nearly moaned at his words. She was all too aware of where his talents did indeed lie. The last thing she needed was that kind of tutelage again. "So, what you're telling me," she said in a smug tone, "is that I have a chance of winning?"

His lips twitched. "Of course," he told her. "Nothing is ever certain."

She nodded. That was true. She could attest to that better than anyone. Life had a way of throwing a person through a loop when they least expected it. She thought she'd be married to the Earl of Moreland for the rest of her life. A fact she hadn't been too happy about, but she never would have believed her husband would die so young. Fate was a funny thing, and now she had the enigmatic, gorgeous duke at her side. If she let herself wish, she'd wish for him. But that wasn't her destiny, no matter how much she wanted it to be. "Then I do believe it is your turn, Your Grace."

He leaned down and said, "All in good time, my lady." The duke nodded toward the bow in her hand. "Let me help you."

She lifted her brow. "You want me to shoot again?"

"Consider the first one…" He paused a moment and then said, "A practice shot. I would hate to win because you're haven't had ample time to hone your skill."

What was he planning? "If you win, what boon will you ask for?"

She didn't know what she wanted. No, that wasn't true. Eden knew exactly what she wanted from him, but didn't think she would ever dare to ask for it. She wanted him to kiss her. Kiss her like he had that night and remind her what true passion could be if she let herself go.

He nodded toward the bow. "Lift it up."

It didn't escape her notice he didn't tell her what he hoped to gain from her. She did as he asked. He came to stand behind her and helped her adjust the bow, then leaned down a little. "Do you see how it lines up?"

Eden nodded. She couldn't speak now if she

wanted to. Having him so close brought all her memories to the surface. Her stomach rolled with so much desire it nearly consumed her.

"Good," he said. His mouth was so close to her ear she could feel his breath wash across her skin with each word he spoke. "Now take a deep breath and blow it out slowly."

Eden did as he instructed. It didn't help. All she wanted to do was drop the bow, turn to him, throw her arms around his neck, and demand he kiss her. "Take one again," he told her. She could barely concentrate with him brushing up against her. Eden could feel every hard inch of him. She wanted to groan and push against him. "When you let out your breath, release the arrow." She did as he instructed. Not because she'd heard him, but because it was an instinctual thing. She let the arrow fly, and it hit the target as if she had actually aimed for it. That hadn't been what had happened at all. Apparently, providence was indeed on her side, after all.

"Perfect," he said. She glanced up at him and she had a feeling he wasn't talking about her shot at all. His gaze was heated and hadn't looked anywhere near the target. His full attention was on one thing, and one thing alone. Her. It was a heady thing and stole her breath. She had to put some distance between them, and fast.

Otherwise, she might start a scandal. One she wouldn't be able to brush aside and move through society with... One she desperately wanted to succumb to, regardless of the consequences. With great strength of will, she stepped away from him and said, "Now it is your turn, Your Grace."

She walked over to Roslyn and Portia and stood with them. Eden would have to settle for watching the duke. Being so close to him was a temptation she could not afford to give in to.

Ten

Eden had decided to go riding. By herself. That was, without anyone around to distract her. Especially one seductive duke that made her burn from the inside out, and that was without him touching her. If he did… She closed her eyes and took several deep breaths. One touch from that man made her want things she had no right to. But oh, how she wished she did…

He'd won the boon at archery. Of course he had… She hadn't thought she'd actually win. What frightened her was that he hadn't asked for his boon yet, and she didn't like that one bit. What if he asked her for something she couldn't give him? Or…what if he asked for something she desperately did want to give him? She wasn't sure which would be worse… Hell, she was starting to suspect both of those options were the exact same thing. Eden wanted to throw herself into his arms and beg him to bring her to the brink of ecstasy over and over again.

She stood next to the mounting block, waiting for one of the stable hands to help her onto the horse. Once she was safely in her saddle, she pressed her knee into the horse and flipped the reins. Before long, she was galloping through a nearby field with the wind whipping around her. This was exactly what she'd needed. It was a boost of freedom that reminded her of everything she'd gained once her husband had died.

She had never wished for his death, but she wasn't so foolish as to ignore what his demise had done for her. It hurt Roslyn far more than it ever would Eden. Roslyn still needed to find a husband. Eden didn't wish to ever marry again. It was enough for her to have her life back and choices she'd never been afforded before.

She slowed her horse to a walk and decided to ride along a trail that led into the woods nearby. Exploring more of the Wyndam estate seemed more appealing than returning for whatever enter-tainments had been planned for the guests. She stopped when she reached a pond. Did she dare dismount and explore more around her? What if she couldn't get back on her horse? No, she couldn't do it. It would be beyond imprudent, and Eden tried to be smart about all her decisions.

Eden sighed and decided to turn around and return. Clouds had started to form overhead, and she feared they were in for a storm. A loud *crack* echoed around her, and her horse whinnied at the sound. The mare hadn't liked it one bit and reared back sharply, causing Eden to slide from its back. She landed on the ground hard. Pain filled her hip, and she cried out as the pain ripped through her.

The beat of hooves on the ground caught her attention. It wasn't her horse, but another nearby. Her horse, the ninny, wandered over to the pond and began to drink. The other rider came into the clearing and stopped when he noticed Eden on the ground. "What are you doing?"

She glared at the duke. Why was he so bloody handsome? "I thought I'd take a break and inspect the grass over here. It looked like a lovely place to sit." Her sarcasm spilled out of her before she had time to stop herself.

His lips twitched. "Is that so?" He slid off his

horse with more ease than anyone should have. "Do you mind if I join you?"

Why was he out riding? She'd gone out hoping to avoid another encounter with him. Had he known she'd be out this way? How could he possibly have known? "I certainly cannot stop you, if that is what you're asking." She could barely move. The pain in her hip was excruciating. Eden didn't think she could ride back to the estate, and walking? She nearly groaned at the thought.

He narrowed his gaze. "You're not telling me something."

There was a lot she wasn't telling him. "I can't imagine what that might be." And she hoped neither could he…

"Are you hurt?" he asked in a soft, soothing tone. Had he noticed that she winced whenever she moved? "Tell me what happened, love."

Why did he insist on using endearments with her? It gave her hope when it was the last thing she could afford to have. "It's nothing." She tried to brush off the accident.

"I doubt that." He leaned down and lifted her into his arms. "Let me take care of you."

Her heart melted a little at his words. It wasn't his fault she had trouble trusting men. He'd been good to her. Always. Even that night when he didn't know her name, and still didn't realize how they were connected. "I don't think I can," she said in a low tone. "I wish I could."

The duke frowned. Rain started to fall from the sky. Lightly at first, then the heavens opened up and drenched them completely. He shook his head and water sprayed even more around them. He was a handsome man, but wet, good lord he was a sight. He chose to ignore her last words. "We need to get out of this rain."

She couldn't argue with that. "There is nowhere to go."

"That's not true. There is a hunting cabin nearby. I will take you there, then come back to secure the horses."

Eden had no idea there had been a cabin nearby. "All right," she conceded. She couldn't very well walk anywhere in her condition.

The duke carried her to the cabin, which hadn't been far at all. How had she not noticed it before? He opened the door and once they were inside, he set her down gingerly. "I'll start a fire once I return. See if you can find some blankets and get out of your wet clothes. You'll catch your death if you don't dry soon."

Eden doubted that it was that dire, but she didn't want to stay in her wet riding habit. She'd much rather be warm and dry. Instead of stripping it off though, she decided to start the fire herself. She found some dry wood and put it in the hearth, then used the nearby tinderbox to start the fire. Once the flames were crackling against the wood, she decided to remove her wet garments. She found a blanket to wrap herself in and slowly removed her riding habit, winching as pain shot through her with each movement. She'd just wrapped the blanket around herself when the door opened again.

The duke froze once he was inside. His gaze roamed over her. She'd undone her hair and let it fall over her shoulder in wet blonde waves. Eden was naked underneath that blanket. Her insides heated and wetness pooled between her thighs. She wanted him. Desperately.

MAX GROANED. SHE WAS A DELECTABLE SIGHT. GOD help him, he didn't think he could stop himself from kissing her. He strode over to her side and lifted his hand to caress her cheek. She looked so lovely and soft, and he'd never wanted anything as much as he wanted her. "Are you warm?" His voice was husky as he spoke. She'd started the fire on her own, and he was grateful she had known how. Not for himself, but so she would be comfortable. He wanted his wet clothes off too, but didn't want to make her feel uneasy. Max would remain dressed until the rain stopped. Then he'd retrieve the horses while she donned her riding habit again. Until then, he had to try to keep his distance from her.

He moved away from her and went to sit on a wood stool near the fire. He held his hands near the flames and then rubbed them together. Cold and seeped inside and seemed to wrap around his bones…

"Aren't you going to take off your wet clothes?" she asked.

He lifted his gaze and met hers. There was something there, but he couldn't pinpoint what. She had always seemed so familiar to him. Even more so now… Eden was standing before him with nothing but a blanket between them—it was almost as if he'd seen her like this before.

"I don't think that is wise." His voice cracked a little. He'd give anything for a decanter of brandy. It might warm him, and it would give him something else to hold in his hand. He itched to touch her again.

"Perhaps not," she said in a soft tone. "But it is perhaps even more of a risk for you to not remove them. You shouldn't risk illness any more than I should." She lifted a brow, then gestured toward another blanket. "If you're worried I'll take advantage of you, I promise I won't do anything untoward."

His lips twitched. As if he would stop her if she did something that scandalous. "What if I want you to compromise me?"

She tilted her head to the side. "Do you?" Eden took a step toward him. She flicked her tongue over her bottom lip, and he groaned.

"I'd like nothing more," he said in a guttural tone. "But I won't use you like that."

Eden frowned and then turned away from him. What had he said?

"Love…"

She jerked her head up. "I'm not your love."

He stood and headed toward her. She backed away from him, but he kept forward. Her back hit a support beam that was in the middle of the cabin. Her body ached, and that hadn't helped any, but she had other things on her mind as she stared at him. Max lifted his hand and cupped her cheek. She wouldn't look at him, so he placed his thumb under her chin and lifted her face so that their gazes locked. "What if I want you to be?" he asked her.

She stared at him as if she didn't understand his question. "I don't know how to love." Her honesty broke him.

"Of course you do." He leaned down until his lips hovered over hers. "You feel this between us." He lifted her hand and placed it on his chest. "My heart is open to you. Just say the word and we can have everything. Tell me you want me too."

She shook her head. A tear fell down her cheek. He wiped it away. There were shadows in her eyes he wished he could erase. She had walked right into his heart, but he might never be able to convince her to be his. Eden had been through so much in her short life. He wished he could raise the dead just long enough to punish her husband for abusing her trust so thoroughly.

Max had done a lot of things he regretted, but he would never regret falling for this woman. He would never love another. She was it for him. All he had to do was convince her of that fact.

"I'm going to kiss you now," he told her. He could no more stop a kiss from happening than time from moving forward. Max closed the distance between them and slanted his lips over hers. It was a slow, methodical kiss. He was testing her to see how much of him he would accept.

She opened her mouth on a gasp. Eden was as sweet as he imagined, and with each move of his mouth over hers he knew one thing with certainty: this was like coming home. His heart beat for her, and he needed her.

If he could battle all the darkness from her life, he would. He'd do anything for her. She was his reason for breathing. Max pulled her into his arms and deepened the kiss farther. Eden lifted her arms and wrapped them around his neck. Nothing was holding that blanket up, and if he took one step back, it would fall.

God help him. He prayed to whatever god would listen for that blanket to fall. Max wanted to make love to her, and he hoped she wanted that, too. He kept kissing her over and over again, until he lost all track of his surroundings. Finally, good fortune was on his side. The rain, her fall, it all had led to this moment, and he promised he'd savor every second of it. This woman captivated him.

Eleven

Eden barely held the blanket against her. She shook with need and was desperate for this man. How could she have ever believed she would be able to resist him? He was everything she'd always wanted, but never thought she could have. That didn't mean she was a fool, though. He hadn't offered her anything. Not really. He'd been sweet and had said all the right words. Things he probably thought she wanted to hear. Truthfully, some of them she had wanted him to say, but he hadn't made any promises of forever.

She wouldn't make a suitable duchess. Not with the taint of scandal attached to her name. He would want someone that had far more innocence than she could ever present to the *ton*. Eden wished she could break this spell that she'd fallen under. He was her weakness. She couldn't gaze upon him and not want things a true lady wanted. Her desperation for his touch was too much to bear.

He stopped kissing her and brushed the pad of his thumb over her lip. "You're beautiful."

Her heart skipped a beat. Pretty words that meant next to nothing... That was all he offered her, yet it was enough. She didn't expect anything more than that from him. Should she give in and ask him to give her pleasure again? It might be the last time she could feel his hands graze over her heated skin or become lost in the luxury of his kiss. "Are you going to remove those wet clothes?"

He kept staring down at her lips. "If I do, I'm going to love you." He pressed a kiss to her cheek. "I'll give you pleasure until you scream my name, and even that won't be enough. If it takes me minutes, hours, or the rest of our lives, I'm going to savor every inch of you." He leaned down and kissed her neck, then pressed his mouth to her ear. "Say the word, love, and I'll ensure you don't regret it."

She closed her eyes and sucked in a breath. "Sometimes promises are broken," she said in a hoarse tone. "Don't make any you cannot fulfill."

"I am not a boastful man." His breaths heated her skin and sent shivers down her spine. "Rest assured, I do not make claims I cannot deliver."

Eden leaned into him and inhaled his scent. He always smelled so wonderful, like sandalwood and spice. She was so wrong for him, and she prayed he wouldn't regret anything. "I can't be what you need." She had to make him understand. "I…" Her voice broke as she considered her next words. "Another scandal will ruin my family."

"There will be no scandal," he said in a firm tone. "Trust me, love."

Eden wanted to, more than anything, but she also wanted him. She couldn't handle the endearments any longer. "Call me Eden," she insisted. It was a far better word, one that gave her hope she had no right to.

The corner of his lip lifted into a wry smile. "As long as you call me Max." he pressed his lips to hers in a quick kiss. "If we're going to be intimate, we should use our given names. He whispered in her ear, "And I do want to hear you scream my name."

She nearly moaned just from his words. It was time to take action. Eden stepped back and dropped her blanket. He inhaled sharply as his gaze roamed over her naked body. He reached for her, but she stepped out of his reach. "No," she said. "Not until you're as naked as I am." She met his gaze and boldly ordered, "Remove your clothes, Max."

He didn't stop to question her demand. His shirt went first. Max wrenched it free and pulled it over his head and threw it to the side. He was such a beautiful man—all rippled muscles and broad shoulders. Eden wanted to run her fingers over all him and explore every inch of his glorious body. After he yanked his boots off, he pushed his breeches down and she gasped as his manhood sprang free. She'd remembered how large he was, and she licked her lips in anticipation. He hadn't allowed her to taste him before, and she was desperate to now.

Slowly, she took a tentative step toward him. When he went to pull her into his arms, she dropped down before him, not allowing him the control he wanted. It was her turn to do what she wanted. She was inexperienced, but she could figure this out. He'd kissed her and brought her pleasure. When he'd first slipped his tongue in her sensitive folds, she'd gasped in shock. She'd never imagined such an act possible.

"Eden," he groaned as she dipped her head.

She cupped her hand over his hardness and then licked over his tip. He cursed, but didn't stop her. "Bloody hell," he said in a hoarse tone. She sucked him into her mouth and rolled her tongue over the sides, then slid him in and out several times. With each moan he made she got bolder and bolder.

Suddenly, he pulled free and then lifted her into his arms. He carried her over to a nearby settee and settled her down. "You're a vixen," he told her. "God help me. You've humbled me." Then wickedness filled his gaze. "Now let me give you pleasure."

"Max…" She moaned as he dipped his head and licked the sensitive nub between her thighs. She nearly bolted off the settee. He held her legs open and used that talented tongue of his over her core. Max kept licking until she writhed with a need so strong she thought she'd burst from the sheer pleasure of it. He slid his fingers inside her and sucked the bud into his mouth. A gust of pleasure overtook her, and stars exploded behind her eyelids. She might have even screamed as her climax overtook her. Eden couldn't be certain of anything, but her throat was sore. She must have screamed.

He settled over her. His hard length was at her entrance, but he hadn't pushed inside her yet. "Are you with me, love?"

She met his gaze. "Yes, always," she told him. "Come inside me."

Max didn't need any more words. He pushed himself inside, and as he filled her, she felt complete. Happiness overwhelmed her. She hadn't thought she would ever feel an emotion that had eluded her for so long. This man gave her everything. She knew then that she loved him and always would.

There was no room for mistrust, hurt, or insecurities in that moment. As he slid in and out of her, Eden gave into her desire. She gave into her love. When she climaxed again, she held on to him, and this time she remembered screaming his name.

What was she going to do without him? Surely, he wouldn't want her when he realized the truth. She hadn't been honest with him. This was not their first time together. Would he hate her when he remembered? Was this truly the last time she'd ever feel his arms wrapped around her?

MAX WOKE ALONE IN THE CABIN. WHERE HAD EDEN gone? He dressed quickly and went in search of her. He went outside and glanced around. The rain had stopped and must have stopped a while ago. Her horse was also gone. His was still tied where he'd left the stallion. He cursed. Had she run scared? Max didn't really blame her. Their passion had been a bit overwhelming. It had been far greater than he could ever have imagined.

He also realized something else. Something he should have noticed much sooner than today. She was his mystery woman. Was that the reason she had resisted him for so long? Did she believe he'd be mad? If so, she couldn't be more wrong.

Ever since that night, he hadn't been able to forget her. If he had known her identity, he would have gone to her much sooner. He didn't think he'd ever see her again. She had admitted that she never went to the Duke of Sinbrough's masquerades, and would be unlikely to ever attend again. It had been one night and one night only.

He'd accepted those terms. Yes, he'd regretted them when she'd left him without a by-your-leave, but they'd agreed to no promises. No future. Max did not accept that now, and she damn well wouldn't run from him ever again. She had to understand that she was his. *His*. He'd made her promises this time. A promise of a future, of trust, and his heart…

Max smiled. His little widow didn't know it yet, but she would be his duchess. She wanted to avoid a scandal? Well, he would use that to his advantage. If she didn't want the *ton* to know about their time together, both at that masquerade and at the cabin, she'd be his wife.

He wasn't above using that against her if need be. It was far better to ask for forgiveness later. He would have the rest of his life to win her, but he had to claim her first. With a plan in place, he whistled as he rode his horse back to the castle. It didn't take him long to reach the stables. He gave his horse to a stable hand and went to the castle. There was a ball that night, and he planned on waltzing with one Lady Moreland, and by the end of the night, he'd be her betrothed.

He strolled into the castle as one of his friends came down the large staircase. "What has you so happy?"

Max met Crawford's gaze and his grin widened. "What has you so miserable?"

The marquess scowled. "I hate the rain," he told him.

"And why is that?" Max lifted a brow. "It never bothered you before."

"I've never been trapped in a castle with a

plethora of unattached ladies vying for my attention while it poured before." He narrowed his gaze. "Where were you during the storm? You were definitely not in the drawing room."

"I was out riding when the storm hit." He didn't offer any other information. "Why were you with all the ladies?"

"Portia insisted I play charades." He shuddered. "Since I had to play, I convinced Lyonsdale to as well. So at least I wasn't the only one tortured to an inch of my life." Crawford wasn't usually prone to dramatics. He had to wonder what the real issue had been. He couldn't fathom what calamity could have caused him to be on the verge of histrionics. Almost like a female… Max probably shouldn't mention that fact to the marquess. Something told him he'd regret the words if they left his mouth.

Max laughed. "I'm certain it wasn't that terrible."

"No," Crawford said. "It was worse. They insisted on teams again. The only good thing was, I wasn't with Lady Roslyn again. Portia was my partner." He frowned. "For some reason that woman hates me."

"Portia?" Max pushed his brows together in

confusion. "Why would your sister hate you?" Lady Portia didn't normally have a mean spirit.

"No," he said waving his hand dismissively. "Not her. Lady Roslyn. Everything I say puts her on edge." He sighed. "At least that is done. Though I did lose. Portia isn't very good at charades."

Crawford had lost at archery too. "Do you owe Lady Roslyn two boons, then?" He hadn't been there for charades and didn't know what rules had been set in place. He did recall that Eden owed him a boon. One he fully intended to collect later.

"I shudder to think what she is going to demand of me." He closed his eyes and took a deep breath. "This house party is dragging on far too long. When is the wedding again?" He'd never seen his friend so distraught.

"Not for a sennight." Max laughed. "I'm certain you will prevail. Are you going to dress for the ball?" It was a dinner ball. There would be dancing, then dinner, and then more dancing. This ball was exclusively for the guests of the house party. The one before the wedding would be much larger and probably fancier.

"Yes," he said, then groaned. "I have to be there for Portia. Why is my mother insisting she has one final season? She clearly doesn't wish to wed." The marquess dragged his hand through his dark hair, leaving it tussled in the wake of his fingers.

Max shrugged. "I couldn't say. I don't know your mother or your sister all that well." He grinned. "I'll see you at the ball. I need to bathe and dress. I'm soaked to the skin and need to warm my frozen flesh."

The truth was, he was still heated from his love-making with Eden, but he wouldn't tell Crawford that. He did need to bathe and dress for the ball, though. Max left the marquess alone and practically skipped up the stairs. Happiness filled him. She would be his. Forever. He knew it to the depths of his soul. He was going to love her for the rest of their lives, and she would not regret becoming his wife. Max fully intended to ensure she was always happy.

Twelve

den nibbled on her bottom lip. She shouldn't have run from him. Surely he would be angry with her. It was a cowardly thing for her to do, but she'd been afraid. Not of him, but of her own feelings. When he was around, she always felt so much it overwhelmed her. She'd stared at him while he slept, and it had taken everything inside of her not to lean down and press her lips to his. To wake him with a kiss, and demand he make love to her all over again.

She'd remembered everything. From the first time he'd pressed his lips to hers, to the feel of him inside of her as they made love. It wasn't the same as it had been with her husband. She'd never loved him. But with Max... Her heart was his and always would be. Even if she knew deep down, she could never have him. She could never call him hers. She would always be his. There was no other man for her. That was her truth. Everything came back to her past, the scandal that tainted her. He deserved far better than what she could offer him.

"What is bothering you?" Roslyn asked. "You've been skittish ever since you returned after the storm." She narrowed her gaze. "Where were you, anyway? Your riding habit was very wet."

It had been soaked but had dried enough for her to put it back on and return to the castle. Roslyn didn't need to know that, though. "I found shelter and waited for the rain to stop."

Roslyn seemed to accept that. They had just finished dressing for the ball. Eden usually wore darker colors, but Roslyn had convinced her to buy a gown of pale pink. It was so pale it bordered on white. Tiny pink flowers had been embroidered into the skirts and lace of the purest white had been sewn into the bodice. It was a lovely gown, and she felt beautiful wearing it. The maid had wound her hair up into a simple chignon, but some tendrils had escaped and curled against her face.

"What did you do while I was taking shelter

from the storm?" Eden asked. Roslyn had gone quiet.

"We played charades," she said. Her attention had drifted, and Eden couldn't help wondering if she had missed something.

Roslyn wore a soft blue gown that brought out that color in her eyes. Her blonde hair was twisted into a plait and wrapped on top of her head. The curls falling down her back had been intentional, unlike Eden's tumbled ones. "Is something bothering you?"

She didn't answer Eden at first. Slowly, Roslyn turned her gaze toward Eden and said, "Do you believe in love?"

Mere hours ago she would have questioned its existence, much like Roslyn now did. "It does exist," Eden said quietly. "I have witnessed it. Just look at Claudine and Lord Wyndam. Their love is so powerful you can't escape noticing it."

After a few moments Roslyn nodded. "But it's rare, isn't it?" She glanced away as if she didn't actually expect Eden to answer her. "Not everyone is lucky enough to find what they have. Perhaps I am asking for too much."

Eden placed her hand on Roslyn's arm. "Do not settle. Your happiness is far too important to marry a man for the sake of having a husband. Love is something worth waiting for."

"I doubt I'll have love," she said in a quiet tone. "I want a family of my own. You understand that, don't you?"

"I do," she said solemnly. Her son was everything to her, and the best thing to have come from her marriage. "But there is no reason to take the first proposal that comes your way. This is only your first season. Do not make a decision you might come to regret."

She nodded. "I promise I won't."

Eden prayed she had made Roslyn understand that she shouldn't rush into marriage, but somehow, she doubted the girl had truly listened to her. Something had happened, but Eden didn't know what that could be. "Let's go down now." They were both ready, and perhaps dancing might lighten Roslyn's glum mood.

They descended the stairs behind a few other guests and headed toward the ballroom. Roslyn walked toward Lady Portia, leaving Eden alone. She could follow her, but something told her to leave her be. She'd made a friend in Lady Portia, and sometimes a lady needed a good friend. That was what she had with Claudine.

Heat spread through her back, and Eden knew before she turned around who stood behind her. He towered over her and made her feel tiny. She closed her eyes and took several deep breaths. It was time to be brave. It was time to turn around and meet his gaze and accept her fate. She had to tell him the truth.

"You ran from me," he said in her ear. "That was naughty of you, love."

"I thought you liked it when I was naughty," she said in a husky tone. It was outlandish what desire could make her foolish mouth spout. She'd never felt this way before. Like she had a secret, one they shared, and if anyone looked too close it would come to the light. She hadn't wanted to fall in love, but here she was. Foolishly, wonderfully, in love with the Duke of Carrington…

"I do," he reassured her. "But not when it sends you away from me." He placed a hand on her waist, so lightly she almost didn't feel it. "You're playing wicked games, love."

"Am I?" The sheer decadence of their byplay was enough to spread desire pooling through her. "Pray tell, Your Grace, whatever shall we do about it then?"

He chuckled softly, then slowly spun her around

until her gaze met his. The heat in his eyes stole her breath. She'd never dreamed she'd meet somebody like him. One that filled her with desire and spoke to her heart... If she lost him, it would devastate her. She had to fight for him, for their future, but she wasn't certain how.

The duke's lips twitched as he fought a smile. He held a hand out to her and said, "Dance with me."

They had danced before, but they'd acted like virtual strangers then. He hadn't remembered their night together probably still didn't. But he would recall their afternoon in the hunting cabin during the rainstorm. Tentatively, she placed her hand in his. This dance seemed important somehow. As if her future would be decided during the waltz, and she nearly shook from the intensity of it.

MAX HAD A PLAN. ONE THAT HE HOPED WOULD END in the conclusion he wanted. He led Eden to the floor as the first strands of the waltz filled the room. Their first dance had been strained. This one was too, but in a different way. Eden was so tense that, with one wrong move, she'd break in his arms. He had to find a way to loosen her up, or this wasn't going to work.

He slid his arm around her and pulled her close. Much closer than he should, but he couldn't make himself care about the proprieties. She was going to be his wife. All he needed was for her to agree and he'd make it happen. If he could, he'd have back-dated their vows, so she was already his wife. In his mind, she was, but he knew that wasn't within the scope of his power.

She flicked her gaze up to meet his. "Do you think this is wise?"

"Yes," he said in a firm tone. "You're mine, and they're all going to know it."

Eden frowned. "That is presumptuous of you. I don't recall agreeing to be yours."

"You did," he insisted. "When you allowed me to love you earlier today?" He leaned closer and said in her ear. "And our first time." He waited for those words to sink in before he added, "At the masquerade."

She stiffened at his words. "I definitely didn't agree to be yours that night. I'm pretty sure that was only meant to be one night."

"But the rules have changed," he insisted. "There are no masks between us now." He twirled her around the floor until they reached the edge of the ballroom. He pulled her toward the nearby balcony doors and whisked her outside. They needed a little privacy for the next part.

She pulled away from him, but he didn't let her go. He slipped her hand in his and led her down the steps to the nearby garden. They walked in silence until they reached the bench he'd found her on a few days ago near the rose bushes. "Sit," he said.

She did as he asked. The moonlight bathed her in light and emphasized her beauty. He had to make her understand, to make her realize how much she meant to him. "Is there a reason we're out here?"

"I never do anything without a reason," he told her. "Were you ever going to tell me?"

She sighed. "Yes," she said after a few moments. "I had planned on telling you tonight. But it seems I don't need to. How long have you known the truth?"

"I think I've always known," he answered honestly. "It just took making love to you for me to fully accept it." Max kneeled beside her. "I've been taken with you from the first moment I laid eyes on you. I'm still taken with you." He lifted her hand into his. "Do you understand what I'm saying?"

She frowned. "You want me to be your mistress?"

"No," he said. "I would never dishonor you that way." He sighed. "I'm blundering this." Max caressed her cheek. He lifted her hand and kissed her palm. "I need a wife. I was willing to settle for marriage without love, but I don't have to."

"Of course not. I don't recommend a loveless marriage. No one knows more than I do how disastrous that can be."

"I know," he said in a quiet tone. "My niece needs a mother." He had to make sure she understood everything. "So, I decided to find a wife."

"I understand," she said in a quiet tone.

"I don't think you do," he said. He was bumbling this and he had to fix it fast or he might lose her. He would not allow that to happen. He had to make her understand. Max needed her. This wasn't just about finding a wife, a mother for his nice. This was about what they had together. "There was this woman that kept haunting my dreams. So, while I scoured the balls and soirees for a woman I could marry, none of them would do. There was only one woman I wanted, but I didn't know her name or where to find her."

Her mouth fell open. "I'm..." She shook her

head. "I'm speechless. What are you trying to tell me?"

"I'm saying I love you. I think I have always loved you, but I didn't think real love existed. Every time you walk into a room, my gaze gravitates toward you." He wanted to pull her into his arms and kiss her until she was breathless. "Whenever you smile, my heart skips a beat, and when I kiss you, I'm lost. You're my weakness, and there is no other woman I want more than you. Please marry me and let me spend the rest of my life making your every dream come true."

She didn't speak for several seconds. Max's heart beat faster and faster inside his chest, and he feared it might burst from the anxiety spreading throughout him. Then she spoke so quietly he almost didn't hear her. "I love you too."

"Say that again," he demanded.

Her lips wobbled as she smiled. "I love you," she said again. "And yes, I'll marry you."

He met her gaze and ordered, "Tell me the truth. Why didn't you tell me that you were the lady from the masquerade sooner?"

Eden smiled up at him and said, "Because a lady never tells." Her lips twitched. "Unless she hopes to start a scandal, and I most certainly wanted to avoid that." She leaned her head against his chest. "I'm lucky, Your Grace, that you're not a perfect gentleman or we'd never have found our way back to each other."

"I'm the lucky one," he said. "Because I have you."

Max didn't wait one second longer to kiss her. He pulled her into his arms and pressed his lips to hers. The kiss between them stole his breath and passion ignited between them. Only this woman made him feel this deeply. He was blessed to have found her, and he would never take her, or her love, for granted. And as far as that boon she still owed him…as far as he was concerned, he already had the best gift she could give him, her love. There was no need for anything else. He had her, and that was enough.

Thank you so much for taking the time to read my book.

Your opinion matters!

Please take a moment to review this book on your favorite review site and share your opinion with fellow readers.

www.authordawnbrower.com

A Lady Never Confesses

LADY BE WICKED BOOK TWO

Continue to the next book in Lady Be Wicked

Lady Roslyn Barrett's launch into society was delayed by her foolish brother's untimely demise. It makes a lady wish she'd been born an only child… All right, she did love the nitwit, and didn't wish him to die; however, that doesn't negate her irritation. Now she is at a disadvantage and the ton won't let her forget her family's scandalous past. She has a secret though, one that she won't confess under any circumstances: Roslyn has already met the man she wants, but he doesn't appear to return her feelings.

Emmett North, Marquess of Crawford shouldn't desire his best friend's new sister. Well, his wife's sister? Hell, he can't keep track of how they are related, but he knows that she's under his friend's protection. Which makes her off limits. If only he could forget Roslyn, but she's always around, and she has a biting wit that she unleashes on him whenever their paths cross. There is only one solution to stop her acerbic nature…a kiss.

Desire is a force neither of them can ignore, but giving in is something they might both regret. Especially when Emmett's friend and Roslyn's new guardian, the Duke of Carrington discovers their scandalous relationship. A confession of love might be their only salvation.

Order here: https://books2read.com/Aladyneverconfesses

Acknowledgments

Special thanks to Elizabeth Evans. Your encouragement and assistance with this book helped me immensely. I am grateful for all you do for me.

About Dawn Brower

USA TODAY Bestselling author, DAWN BROWER writes both historical and contemporary romance. There are always stories inside her head; she just never thought she could make them come to life. That creativity has finally found an outlet.

Growing up, she was the only girl out of six children. She raised two boys as a single mother; there is never a dull moment in her life. Reading books is her favorite hobby, and she loves all genres.

www.authordawnbrower.com
TikTok: @1DawnBrower

bookbub.com/authors/dawn-brower

facebook.com/1DawnBrower

x.com/1DawnBrower

instagram.com/1DawnBrower

goodreads.com/dawnbrower

Loving an America Spy

Linked Across Time

Saved by My Blackguard

Searching for My Rogue

Seduction of My Rake

Surrendering to My Spy

Spellbound by My Charmer

Stolen by My Knave

Separated from My Love

Scheming with My Duke

Secluded with My Hellion

Secrets of My Beloved

Spying on My Scoundrel

Shocked by My Vixen

Smitten with My Christmas Minx

Vision of Love

Enduring Legacy

The Legacy's Origin

Charming Her Rogue

Ever Beloved

Forever My Earl

Always My Viscount

Infinitely My Marquess

Eternally My Duke

Bluestockings Defying Rogues

When An Earl Turns Wicked

A Lady Hoyden's Secret

One Wicked Kiss

Earl In Trouble

All the Ladies Love Coventry

One Less Scandalous Earl

Confessions of a Hellion

The Vixen in Red

Lady Pear's Duke

Scandal Meets Love

Love Only Me (Amanda Mariel)

Find Me Love (Dawn Brower)

If It's Love (Amanda Mariel)

Odds of Love (Dawn Brower)

Believe In Love (Amanda Mariel)

Chance of Love (Dawn Brower)

Love and Holly (Amanda Mariel)

Love and Mistletoe (Dawn Brower

The Neverhartts

Never Defy a Vixen

Never Disregard a Wallflower

Never Dare a Hellion

Never Deceive a Bluestocking

Never Disrespect a Governess

Never Desire a Duke

Lady Be Wicked/Wayward Dukes'/Wicked Widows'

Her Rogue for One Night (Wicked Widows)

A Lady Never Tells

Her Duke to Beguile

Her Duke of Sin (Wayward Dukes')

Her Duke to Savor (Wayward Dukes')

Coming in 2024/2025

A Lady Never Confesses

A Lady Never Forgets

Her Rogue for Christmas (Wicked Widows)

Her Rogue to Kiss Good Morning (Wicked Widows)

Her Duke to Seduce (Wayward Dukes')

Her Duke to Tempt (Wayward Dukes')

CONTEMPORARY

Stand alone:

Deadly Benevolence

Snowflake Kisses

Kindred Lies

Sparkle City

Diamonds Don't Cry

Hooking a Firefly

Novak Springs

Cowgirl Fever

Dirty Proof

Unbridled Pursuit

Sensual Games

Christmas Temptation

Daring Love

Passion and Lies

Desire and Jealousy

Seduction and Betrayal

Begin Again

There You'll Be

Better as a Memory

Won't Let Go

Heart's Intent

One Heart to Give

Unveiled Hearts

Heart of the Moment

Kiss My Heart Goodbye

Heart in Waiting

Heart Lessons

A Heart Redeemed

YOUNG ADULT FANTASY

Broken Curses

The Enchanted Princess

The Bespelled Knight

The Magical Hunt

www.ingramcontent.com/pod-product-compliance
Lightning Source LLC
Chambersburg PA
CBHW021200160726
47994CB00001B/303